Life, Death & Cricket

Sherin Nair

First published in India 2015 by Frog Books
An imprint of Leadstart Publishing Pvt Ltd
1 Level, Trade Centre
Bandra Kurla Complex
Bandra (East) Mumbai 400 051 India
Telephone: +91-22-40700804
Fax: +91-22-40700800
Email: info@leadstartcorp.com
www.leadstartcorp.com / www.frogbooks.net

Sales Office:
Unit No.25/26, Building No.A/1,
Near Wadala RTO,
Wadala (East), Mumbai - 400037 India
Phone: +91 22 24046887

US Office:
Axis Corp, 7845 E Oakbrook Circle
Madison, WI 53717 USA

ISBN 978-93-52013-30-2

Book Editor: Sharanya Nair
Design Editor: Mishta Roy
Layout: Logiciels Info Solutions Pvt. Ltd.

Typeset in Book Antiqua
Printed at Dhote Offset Technokrafts Pvt. Ltd., Mumbai

Price – India: Rs 125; Elsewhere: US $ 5

Dedication

Dedicated to

Cricket,

A billion cricket-crazy countrymen,

And Sachin for carrying the hopes of all those billions.

About the Author

Dr. Sherin Nair is a dentist by profession with a passion for storytelling. He is an alumni of GDC, Calicut where he was the College Union Editor, which was his first brush with writing of any kind. After completing his masters in Oral Pathology from the same college, Dr. Sherin joined a dental college in Calicut as a lecturer. Presently, he is an Asst. Professor in Kothiwal dental college, Moradabad, UP. He lives in Moradabad with his wife Simi, an ex-classmate, and his daughter Niharika.

Author's Note

A story may mean different things to different people but I consider this book a tribute to two things. First, is the unending love us Indians have for cricket. When a country of over a billion people comes to a standstill on the eve of a cricket match, you have to wonder and marvel at the phenomenon into which this game has turned. Across all the differences of caste, creed and politics, cricket is the one religion that binds us all. Hence, hats off to the beautiful game and all its followers.

Second, and equally important, is the work of the Palliative Care Society. For those of you who are not aware, palliative treatment is a relatively new branch of medicine concerned primarily with pain relief and other supportive measures. The patients are mostly those afflicted with terminal cancer or other similar debilitating and generally incurable conditions. The aim of palliative medicine is to provide such patients with relief from pain and improve their quality of life, however brief it may be.

The Pain and Palliative Care Society in Calicut is at the forefront of palliative treatment in India. During my internship, I had a chance to be a part of their work and learn from them. One person who made a deep impact on me then was Dr. Suresh sir who is the head of this institution. In an era when even the noble practice of medicine is in the grips of commercialization and money mindedness, Dr. Suresh and his team are a beacon of selfless service to all of us in the same field. Consider this book a humble dedication to them for upholding the ideals upon which our profession was built.

Lastly, I would like to mention that this story is purely a work of fiction even though some of the characters, events and places are quite real. The timeline of the Indian cricket teams overseas tours mentioned in the story has been changed to before the World Cup, when in reality they took place after it. Consider this and any other transgressions that you may note as creative liberty on my part to bring you a more engaging story experience.

Acknowledgements

It's been a bittersweet journey with this book of mine. And I have been fortunate enough to be accompanied on this journey by my friends and family. Hence, the book, in part atleast, belongs to all those people. The list is probably endless, but I will try to keep it short.

God, who - for reasons I still can't fathom - chose me as the medium to bring you this story.

My better half, Simi, who prodded and pushed my lazy self to take writing seriously. Thank you, Simi, for believing in me.

My little girl, Ammu for coming into my world and showing me the wonders of childhood. Seeing her persistence for getting even a small bar of chocolate and the joy at getting it made me realize what kids have and what we as adults lack - appreciating the simple pleasures of life.

- My family for their constant support and encouragement.
- My friends, both new and old. Special mention has to be made of my college buddies, particularly, Raman,

Frency and Rakesh. For some bizarre reason, they made me the College Editor, which literally forced me into writing.

- My teachers and colleagues from Calicut and now in Moradabad.
- Dr. Auswaf Ahsan and Dr. Anoop. My dearest colleagues and the best of friends and advisors.
- To all my students who over the years have probably taught me more about life than I have about dentistry to them.
- My publishers, Leadstart Corp. for giving me this opportunity.
- The entire editorial team, including Mr. Swarup Nanda, Mr. Omkar Thakur, Ms. Sharanya Nair, Malini Nair and all the others who have made this book a reality.
- Finally, you the readers who have picked up this book and hopefully will like it.

Chapters

Prologue

Sam had very simple tastes. He liked chocolates and ice creams and chocolate ice-cream. It was difficult to say which among the three he liked best. The same was the case with Fawad, more or less. He, however, was very clear about what he liked *best*. It was ice creams; but that opinion was prone to change every week or two.

Both of them were clueless as to their career options. Of all the infinite possibilities, Sam was currently focused on being a truck driver. According to him, it allowed him to play with big engines, get respect (the bigger the vehicle, the better the respect) and travel the whole world (even to America). Fawad only got the bit about getting respect and so decided that he would drive the biggest vehicle around, a rocket. Hence, he wanted to be an "astronut". Sam tried to correct him, but nothing could convince Fawad to be anything but a "nut".

They were united in their dislike of girls; the weird appearance and habits were difficult to understand and they were divided on the reasons for these differences. Sam believed that it was a simple case of a manufacturing defect. Fawad was convinced that girls were from another planet, specifically Venus (he had read so on a book once).

Sam liked Ben10. Fawad liked the i10. Sam knew that the Prime Minister was bigger than the President, because it sounded bigger. Fawad pooh-poohed this claim. According to him, the most powerful person was the Member of Parliament.

They did agree on certain things though. India could kick America's ass on any given day; the television was not an idiot box as everyone said; and aiming for the opposite wall while peeing was an art unto itself.

There were only two things in this world of which they were thoroughly convinced: one, they were the best friends in the world; and two, Sachin was the greatest cricketer in the whole universe.

They did have one more thing in common; they were both terminal cancer patients.

****

A Not So Bright Future

"We have tried every possible treatment for him. This is all that's left to do."

Mr. Martin sat stunned for a moment. The very last iota of hope that he still had was drained by the words of Dr. Rao. *How did it come to this? How could Sam, his little boy, be dying? He was only twelve, for Christ's sake.*

"Dr. Rao, I can take him to any place in this world. He shall get the best possible care that medicine has to offer. I will get my son back. He will not die just because his father gave up on him," Mr. Martin declared defiantly.

Dr. Rao had seen all of this and much more in his 30-year long career. He had saved some and lost some during this time. With most other fields of medicine, you could act like a machine and call it professionalism. Losing a patient would not be a big issue there. But Pediatrics was different. And Pediatric Oncology was particularly taxing, both for the body and spirit. Dealing with a dying kid was an ordeal in itself. Equally demanding was the job of handling the family and their reactions. It was denial in this case.

"Mr. Martin, as opposed to popular perception, India is one of the best centers in the world as far as cancer treatment is concerned. If taking Sam to US or UK or anywhere else could save him, I myself would have suggested so. The best thing that you can do for him now is to support him and let him go in peace."

"How is a palliative care centre going to help," asked Mr. Martin.

"A palliative care centre will be able to manage Sam's day-to-day needs much better than you could at home. This is going to become more important as his disease worsens and his medical needs increase. It might give him some more time and, more importantly, will improve his quality of life and ease any pain."

Dr. Rao continued, "This city has one of the best palliative centers in the world. I will refer you to Dr. Senthil there, who is a friend of mine. He will explain the details to you."

"Doctor, if there's any other way…" Mr. Martin persisted.

"We all have Sam's best interests at heart; and this is what's best for him at this stage."

Mr. Martin slowly got up and opened the door; halfway out he glanced back and said, "Doctor, keeping his best interests at heart, let's spare Sam the truth."

Mr. Martin slowly opened the door to his son's room. He had hoped to find him asleep so as to avoid uncomfortable questions. But Sam was tapping away at his gaming console. *Stupid video games*, he thought.

"Hey kid. Looks like we will be out of here sooner than expected," said Mr. Martin with a cheerfulness he did not feel.

"Really, dad? So I am going to be fine?" asked Sam.

"Sure. We will move to a new hospital for a few days and then you will be up and running in no time."

"But dad, I want to go home. Tony will have wrecked my room by now."

"Oh, don't you worry. Your room is fine and off limits as far as Tony is concerned. This new hospital is especially for kids. You will meet lots of new friends there, get better soon and then, back home." Mr. Martin said.

"OK, then. Let's go there." Sam was up and ready.

"Not now. In a few days' time, after I have settled a few things here."

Mr. Martin left after some time, citing some official business. Sam watched his dad leave and burst into tears soon after. His father could fool others but not him. Quite contrary to what his dad believed, Sam knew everything about his disease and its ultimate outcome. The internet was a storehouse of information, even the not very pleasant kind. The look in his father's eyes was, however, all the info that he needed.

A good cry every now and then can do wonders for your spirit. Sam realized this an hour or so later as he sat contemplating his not so bright future.

So this is it, he thought. *He wouldn't be able to buy his Ferrari after all. Nor would he be around for flying cars and robotic servants. Living on the moon was also out of the question.* A tinge of jealousy crept in as he thought of Tony. *The little idiot would get to see and do all this and much more.*

All was not lost though. The highlight was, of course, no school. An evil grin spread across his face as he thought of the no-school-all-play season ahead of him, coupled with the all-school-no-play life ahead for Tony. Plus, if he played the sick card properly, he could gobble up more ice cream in the time left than Tony could in his entire lifetime. If he was lucky enough, he'd get to see Sachin in action at the World cup. That would be great.

Let's check out this new place first. Hope it has TV and stuff. Maybe I will make some new friends as dad says, even if it was only for a short time. Sam drifted off to sleep.

****

New Place and New Friends

The big white and red building loomed in front of him as Sam made his way past the gates, accompanied by his mom and dad. '**Pain and Palliative Care Centre, Calicut**', proclaimed the golden plaque in front of the building. *Hope it's not as depressing and gloomy as it seems from the outside,* thought Sam as he stepped into the hospital.

The preliminary admission procedures over, Sam checked into his room into the Pediatrics wing of the hospital. He did manage to catch a glimpse of some other children at the far end of the corridor, but couldn't get to meet them as his dad insisted on settling down in the room first. Sam too was tired from the journey and soon fell asleep.

An hour or so later, he woke up, just as Dr. Senthil entered his room. He was the head of the institute as well as the resident pediatrician. The guy seemed cheerful enough despite the perpetual cloud of death looming over his wards. He gave Sam a thorough check-up, read his files, babbled something that sounded like Greek to the accompanying nurse and then dashed off after giving Sam a pat on the shoulder.

Just as Dr. Senthil was out of the room, something, or rather *someone,* came running down the corridor and dashed into him from behind. Sam opened his door and saw Dr. Senthil lying in a heap on the floor. The culprit was a small boy of around ten or twelve who was now standing with his head bowed in shame.

"Fawad, my boy, you will have to do better than that to kill me," muttered Dr. Senthil as he got up and dusted himself off. Being knocked out by a kid was embarrassing enough but he tried to laugh it off instead of taking it out on the poor kid.

"Sorry, Doctor Uncle, but it was Raju. He was trying to snatch my chocolate," complained the boy.

"Was he now? I will surely poke him with an extra needle the next time for such a heinous crime," said the good humored doctor before adding, "Where's your chocolate by the way? Won't you share it with doctor uncle?"

The boy, Fawad, was now on the verge of tears. "I dropped it on the run," he said with a slight sob.

"Don't you worry! Here's one from doctor uncle. Finish it off before Raju sees it," said Dr. Senthil as he produced a Cadbury's from his coat, handed it to Fawad and resumed his rounds.

The sob turned into cheerful glee in the blink of an eye. As soon as the doctor turned the corner, Fawad pocketed his gift and called out, "Ok, come on out and pay up. I haven't got all day."

Sam gazed in amazement as a horde of kids emerged from the other end of the corridor and gathered around Fawad. One by one, they all handed over more chocolates to him, which he duly stuffed into his pockets.

An irritated voice called out from the far end, "Fawad, how many times have I told you not to wander around like this! My goodness, this kid will drive me nuts one day," muttered the lady, presumably Fawad's mom, as she made her way towards him. The crowd of kids disappeared as soon as it had formed, leaving only Fawad standing with a sheepish grin and bulging pockets.

"I should ask doctor uncle to tie you down to your bed. But then you will probably drag the bed along with you. What are you doing here anyway?" Fawad's mom had a stern look on her face.

Just then Fawad spotted the new inmate standing by the door. "I was down here to see our newest guest. I wanted him to feel at home here and offer my help, anytime he needed it. Anyway, *Ammi*, this is...," Fawad hung back and hoped that the new guy could take the cue.

"Sam," the new guy did take the cue.

"Sam! Hi, Sam. Ammi, meet Sam. Sam, this is my Ammi; and I am Fawad." He held out his hand.

"Glad to meet you," said Sam as he took Fawad's hand.

Sam's parents had also seen most of this drama unfold from the doorway. Fawad's mom straightened up as she saw them and the adults exchanged a few pleasantries.

"I am sorry about Fawad. He is a certified public nuisance," Ammi said with a smile.

"You still love me though." Fawad was sucking up to Ammi, to avoid any probable thrashing later on.

"That's no problem at all. He seems a cute little kid. In fact, Sam here is no better," said Sam's mom.

"Well, we should get going. It's time for his lunch," said Ammi as she began to drag Fawad away. "We'll see you around. Bye, *beta,*" she said with a pleasant smile as she gave Sam a slight peck on his cheek.

"See you, Sam," said Fawad as he too gave Sam a peck on his cheek mockingly. But then he drew him closer still and whispered "thank you," before discreetly handing over two chocolates from his stuffed pockets.

Sam looked at the gift and then back at the kid as he frolicked behind his Ammi, bouncing up and down as he went.

Strange little kid; will be good time-pass though, with him around, thought Sam.

Strange kid; should provide another avenue for chocolates, thought Fawad.

And that is how they first met…

****

Later in the evening, Sam sat on his bed playing one of his video games. He had promised his mom and dad that he wouldn't stay up late and, as usual, had no intention of following up on it. The hospital policy did not allow visitors or relatives to stay back, and so his parents were staying with one of their relatives in the city. Sam was thankful for this as he could not bear to see his mom silently sobbing away. He could also fully immerse himself into the mission of destroying all the alien forces thereby pushing any thoughts of dying into the background.

His door suddenly creaked and a small head poked in from the narrow opening. "Mind if I come in?" Fawad was already in the room, not waiting for the answer.

"Did you like my chocolates?" Fawad asked with a smile.

"They are there on the table," Sam answered with slight irritation; his mission was hanging unfinished.

"Why? Don't you like them?" Fawad obviously didn't understand that he was not welcome.

"I do; but I am not supposed to eat them as they will rot my teeth."

"Says who? Look at me; I eat loads of them but my teeth are still pearly white." Fawad said as he showed off his pearly whites. He jumped up onto the bed alongside Sam and continued talking.

"It must be doctor uncle who told you that. He says the same thing to every kid here, even to me. And everyone believes it to be true, coming from the mouth of a doctor. But I have actually tested his opinion and found it to be absolutely baseless. The guy has another agenda going on - not at all concerned with the good health of our teeth."

By this time, Sam knew that Fawad had no intention of leaving anytime soon. So he put aside his video game and sat upright preparing himself for an evening of Fawad's ranting.

"What other agenda?" Sam asked as he tucked in a pillow between his legs.

Fawad moved in closer and whispered in a conspiratorial voice, "Kamala sister tells me that doctor uncle has sugar and so can't have chocolates himself. Hence, he is jealous of everybody else who can and advises them not to. He is a scheming villain out to rid the world of chocolates."

"My God! Fortunately for us, we have a brave hero in you. All his schemes will bite the dust with you around." Sam's words dripped with satire.

"That's true," Fawad said as he eyed Sam's video game. The satirical part was totally lost on him.

"What was that business with doctor uncle earlier today?"

"It was a bet. I won, as always."

"You mean you bumped into him on purpose!! Why ...what for?"

"For this," said Fawad as he showed off the spoils of his mission. "I even managed to get one from the victim himself. Two dogs with one stone."

"I think it is two birds," suggested Sam.

"Birds, dogs ...doesn't matter. What matters is that now I am stocked up for the whole week. What is that thing, by the way?" Fawad was pointing to the video game.

"It's my gaming console. Don't you have one?"

"Nope; Ammi says that playing video games is bad for your brain ...reduces IQ or PQ or something."

Sam was incredulous, "No it doesn't. How can you believe such a thing?"

"Ammi always speaks the truth."

"Why don't you test your Ammi's theory like you did with doctor uncle's?" Sam handed his video game to Fawad. "With your high IQ, it won't matter even if she is true and you do happen to lose some."

Fawad was slightly skeptical as he took the thing from Sam. The skepticism changed to interest in the next five minutes. An hour or so later, he was lost in the land of aliens and rockets and planes. Unfortunately, the batteries ran out and he had to return back to earth. Sam meanwhile was engrossed in one of his comics.

"This is awesome. Ammi was definitely wrong about video games," Fawad said as he handed the thing back to Sam. "Well, it's pretty late now. You get some rest and then tomorrow I will show you around the hospital and introduce you to the other guys. We have a busy day ahead. Goodnight, Sam." Fawad said as he headed out the door.

"Goodnight then. See you tomorrow," Sam said through half-shut eyes.

****

A Deadly Cold

The promise of a busy day was not to be as Fawad was not seen around for the whole day – and the next couple of days as well. Sam hated to admit it but he was missing the pesky little one. And so he decided to pay Fawad a little visit.

"Hi there, friend," Sam called out as he entered Fawad's room. He was horribly pale and could barely open his eyes, but Fawad managed a weak smile back, "Come on in, Sam."

"Didn't see you around for a couple of days. So I thought that you must has left," said Sam as he seated himself by the bed. Ammi was doing something by the table and Sam acknowledged her with a smile.

"Nope, I have been down with this blasted cold," said Fawad as he propped himself up.

"Our tour of the hospital is still on, right?"

"Definitely! I will be back in action by tomorrow. That's how long it normally takes for the cold to subside."

"So what exactly is wrong with you? Why are you here anyway?"

"Because of the cold, dumbo. I get it from time to time." Fawad was amazed that Sam couldn't grasp something so obvious.

"That's ridiculous. Nobody gets admitted for a simple cold."

"Oh, but this is not just any cold. It a very deadly variety of cold … like the bird flu. That's why I need to be here so that they can treat it immediately, right Ammi?" Fawad looked to his mom for confirmation.

"Yes, son," smiled Ammi weakly before quickly turning away. Sam was however able to see the tears in her eyes and understood their meaning.

"What are you in here for? You don't have the deadly cold, do you?" asked Fawad.

"No, I have Leukemia." Sam's answer was simple and short.

"See, now that's a pretty cool-sounding disease. If you are going to be admitted, you should be admitted for that. Not for some stupid cold. Wish I too could have Leukemia," sighed Fawad.

"Fawad..." Ammi suddenly turned around with a look of anger and dismay on her face. A second later she dashed out of the room covering her face with the *dupatta.*

"Don't know what all that was about... "Fawad was confused.

"Don't worry. She will be fine in a short while," said Sam. "I should go now. I'll come in the evening to get this back," Sam said as he took out the video game from his bag and handed it to Fawad.

"Yay! Thank you, man. I will get better much faster with this around," Fawad said as he snatched the thing from Sam. The sleepiness and tiredness were gone in an instant.

"Get some rest. See you later," said Sam as he left Fawad with the video game and his deadly cold.

****

As promised, Fawad was back in form by the next day. He attributed this in no small measure to the miraculous effect of Sam's video game – with the result that Ammi was coaxed into buying a similar one for him. This lifted his already buoyant spirits even higher as he skipped along happily to meet Sam.

"Hey Sam, I am back," he called out as he entered his room.

Sam was being force-fed the most horrible thing in this whole world – vegetables. He was sick of the green stuff and on the verge of hurling in a bad way. Grateful for Fawad's grand entry, he quickly grabbed at the opportunity with both hands.

"Hey Fawad, ready for our tour?"

"Sure thing, buddy. Finish up your meal and then we can go and harass the poor souls of this hospital."

"Oh, I am more than finished," Sam said in a dreary voice.

"No, no … there's some more left. You have to eat all of it to keep up your health," protested his mother as she tried to push another spoonful down his throat.

"Mom, if I eat any more of that, whatever health I still have will also be gone," said Sam as he twisted his head away from the dreaded spoon.

"It's not all that bad. Here Fawad, why don't you try some," said Sam's mom as she extended the spoon out to Fawad.

Fawad took one look at the thing and involuntarily took two steps backwards. He didn't want to be rude to Sam's mom and so took to the most diplomatic option available. "Thanks Aunty, but I just had my lunch," he said and rubbed his tummy to indicate an already full stomach.

Sam jumped in to rescue Fawad. "Mom, he has just recovered from a deadly cold. Please don't make him sick again," he said as he grabbed Fawad by the hand and ran out the door. "We will have the rest of it later. Bye" he called out as he closed the door behind him.

His mother looked on helplessly towards the door for a second and then threw away the rest of the veggies into the dust bin. She knew too well that when Sam said 'later', it usually meant never. She couldn't fault him though; she herself would never eat that stuff unless she was being force-fed by her mom.

****

"Thanks for saving me back there," Sam said as he dragged Fawad along the corridor. He wanted to get away from his room as fast as possible.

"What did you mean by 'we' will have it? I wouldn't eat that stuff even if it was the last available thing on earth," said Fawad as he struggled to keep pace with Sam.

"A good friend is one who accepts a friend's troubles as his own," Sam said in a half-mocking voice.

"Sounds nice but doesn't apply in this situation. In fact, I won't be coming anywhere near your room when your mom is around."

"Relax, I was just joking. Mom knows me only too well. We won't have to suffer vegetables again." Sam playfully poked Fawad in the ribs and ran off.

"Again with the 'we'!" Fawad said in mock anger as he dashed after him.

Dr. Senthil was coming up the stairs from the opposite direction. As soon as he saw the two kids running towards him, he quickly made way and flattened his considerable bulk against the wall. He obviously didn't want a repeat of the previous incident with Fawad.

"So Fawad, you are up and running again. I should probably put out a warning for everyone!" The doctor was in a jovial mood.

"Doctor uncle," Fawad stopped to catch his breath "I was just showing Sam around the hospital."

"You are just about out of bed rest. Why don't you take it a bit slow for some time? You know, walking like normal people, instead of sprinting around." The doctor turned to Sam, "And you, Sam, seems you are the newest addition to this circus brigade I am running here."

Fawad jumped in, "On the contrary, I was just telling Sam about this wonderful hospital. Such neatness, such orderliness, such…" Fawad was at a loss for more superlatives.

"*Butteringness*?" suggested Dr. Senthil with a knowing smile on his face. He was not going to fall into Fawad's trap.

"Such *butteringness!*"Fawad didn't understand the word but probably took it for some complicated medical terminology. "And all this is possible only because of doctor uncle. Without his brilliant leadership, this hospital would be totally lost. Like a chocolate cake without chocolate, like a ..."

"Fine, fine!" The doctor stepped in before Fawad went overboard with the buttering. "Here's your chocolate." He handed Fawad two pieces and went on his way.

"You really are something else," Sam looked on in awe as Fawad gobbled one of the chocolates up immediately. He graciously gave the other to Sam.

"I am a genius," Fawad managed to speak through a mouthful of sticky mass.

The rest of the tour went on in more or less similar fashion. They met up with the other kids in the ward, harassed Velan - the sweeper - by deliberately walking along the areas he had scrubbed and sucked up to the nurse aunties because they controlled the needles.

"And this is our common recreation room," Fawad said as he led Sam into a large hall. The room had a small play area with slides and rocking chairs, a carom board, a chess board and other assorted indoor games and also a reading area with books and magazines. It even had a table tennis table lying at the far end -more or less everything that a recreation room was supposed to have. But Sam's eyes were riveted on the TV screen placed almost exactly in the center of the room. Not because it was a next generation huge LED or plasma TV but because of the person he now saw on it.

It was Sachin – hitting boundary after boundary. One of the sports channels was proudly displaying all of his centuries so far, for the sake of the cricket crazy Indian masses. The channel knew that a program such as this was sure to notch up more TRP's in India than even the most gut wrenching, heartrending soap operas. Judging by the look in Sam's eyes, they were right.

Sam stood transfixed as the Master Blaster sped towards another century. A commercial break brought him back to his senses and he realized that Fawad's incessant chatter was no longer to be heard. Fearing he had gone deaf, he looked around and saw Fawad sitting right in front of the TV screen with his mouth half-open. Sam moved towards him and gently tapped Fawad on the shoulder. He looked up and indicated that Sam join him. The look in both their sets of eyes was enough to reveal to them their shared love for cricket. Without a doubt, the fervor in their eyes had also given away their most favorite cricketer. No words were needed.

Sachin returned after the commercial to demolish more bowlers. Sam and Fawad resumed their silent worship by the TV screen. The guy who had originally been watching the TV soon got up and left, probably because he couldn't change any channels with the two heads now blocking it. Their moms came and said their goodbyes for the evening; Sam and Fawad hardly took notice. When the program finally ended, they got up as though in a trance and walked back to their respective rooms.

The hospital tour never got past the TV and Sachin….

****

Allah and Jesus

It was the darkest day of Fawad's life, the day he finally realized that he too was dying. One of his mates Riyas had been sick for a few days and had passed away the previous night.

"Ammi, am I going to die?" The question was posed suddenly in the midst of a Koran recital his Ammi used to give him.

"Why Fawad, what a silly idea," said Ammi diplomatically dodging the question.

"Riyas, who came to the hospital the same time as me, died yesterday. So did Shreyas and Rani before him. Velan, the sweeper says no one leaves this hospital hale and hearty. If that is true, I too am going the way of my friends." Fawad choked.

Ammi's face almost betrayed her feelings. The sheer helplessness of it! Here she wanted to cry her heart out but couldn't. She looked at her dear boy; the tears on his pale cheeks reminded him of the times when he was so tiny, he could cuddle up and hide in her bosom. She could still try to do that, if it would shield him from what was coming. She was by now somewhat used to living in the shadow of death. This however was the day she had been dreading for some time now. She placed the Koran aside and moved closer to Fawad on the bed, hugging him tightly.

"Fawad, there comes a time when all of us leave this world and go to live in Allah's heaven, which is a much happier place. Those among us dearer to Allah get to go sooner than the rest. You, of course, being Allah's favorite kid will get to meet him very soon." The dam finally burst and Ammi could talk no more.

Fawad realized the implications of what Ammi had just told him. He also understood the meaning of the words "very soon". But with Ammi in tears, he didn't want to add to her grief. He chose to be her brave boy instead.

"Do they have *sewaiyya* and lamb *kebabs* there?"

"Sure they do," Ammi said, wiping away her tears.

"Does Allah have Cartoon Network and video games?"

"He is the master of everything. I am sure he could arrange for that," said Ammi.

"Then I won't mind going there. I should tell Sam about it," chirped Fawad before running off down the corridor. Ammi watched as her son disappeared from view and dreaded the day when he would disappear from her life forever.

****

Death is something difficult to deal with, particularly if it's your own. Ammi's words had only confirmed what Fawad had doubted for some time now. Anyone else in his place would probably have drowned in depression, but not Fawad. His natural buoyant nature and upbeat outlook had him coming to terms with the truth remarkably fast. Soon enough, he was back to his innocent and naïve self.

"Hey Sam, guess what. I am going to Allah's heaven. I will be sitting by his side and playing PlayStation and watching Cartoon network all day." The talk with Ammi had sparked Fawad's imaginative genius.

"Don't you think you will have to go to school?" Sam was out to spoil it for him.

"No silly, they don't have schools in heaven."

"Why so?"

"Because all the teachers are in hell, you dumbo." Fawad's imagination was working overtime now.

"Well I too am bound for heaven. So, looks like we will be there together. Just like here." Sam urged him on.

"Wow! That would be great. We should work out a schedule for the gaming and TV time though," said Fawad before abruptly running out of the room.

Five seconds later, he barged in again, a worried look on his face.

"Sam, I will be in Allah's heaven while you will be in Jesus'. I don't think we can be together there."

"Oh, don't worry. I am sure Jesus and Allah have some working arrangement where they allow friends from both sides to meet from time to time," said Sam to ease Fawad's mind.

"Boy, am I relieved! Heaven will not be the same without you around." And then he was off again.

"I too believe the same, my friend," thought Sam as he watched him leave.

****

Cricket, Sachin and Superstitions

"No, No, No! What is he doing?" Sam blurted out in frustration as they watched the India-Australia match in the common room.

"Looks like he is trying to get out," exclaimed Fawad.

"Thank you, Fawad, for your brilliant observation and expert opinion," Sam retorted angrily. Fawad took the cue and kept his trap shut.

The "He" in question here was Sachin. The Indian team had been on tour for the last couple of months. And they had been handed one defeat after another during this time. First England and now Australia was making short work of the famed Indian batting line-up. More than anyone else's, it was Sachin's failure that hurt the most. The guy had been close to his one-hundredth hundred for quite some time now. But somehow he seemed to lack the energy and will to get there. Sam feared that Sachin was getting tired of cricket.

"He should hit a four. It will help." Fawad's short vow of silence was over.

Sam sighed. Fawad's one-trick solution for all of a batsman's problems was to hit a boundary. Easier said than done! Choosing the right ball, getting the timing and placement right and a number of other factors came into play –a difficult thing to do when one is out of form.

FOUR!

Sachin seemed to have heard Fawad and took his advice to heart. *Well, not too difficult a thing, if you are Sachin Tendulkar,* thought Sam. Fawad did come up with some pearls of wisdom in between truck-loads of stupidity.

"Hey, where are you going," asked Sam as Fawad got up to leave.

"I will just roam around and come back later. I have bribed Kamala sister to smuggle some ice cream for us. Will get it too … on the way back."

"What did you bribe her with? What do you have except for that empty piggy bank?"

"My boyish charm and dashing good looks! Kamala sister will get anything for me in exchange for a smile." Fawad obviously had some wild notions about his looks.

"Yeah, right! You can't leave now. Sachin has started to play well. Come back and sit right where you were sitting, in exactly the same position," Sam was adamant about superstition when it came to cricket.

"But I have to pee," begged Fawad.

"Pee later," Sam the Hitler commanded.

"But this is a Test match. What if the guy plays on all day?"

"Then you will sit here all day. You can pee here itself and say that you have lost control of your bladder. You are a kid, that too a sick one. They will understand." Just like Fawad, in his own way, Sam had a solution for everything.

"Yeah, they will understand. They will also push up a big pipe through my wee-wee with a bag hanging underneath. No thanks, but I will let that golden opportunity pass." Fawad was already on the way out before he had finished speaking.

Right then tragedy struck. "Out!" screamed the commentator and Sam turned back to see Sachin trotting back across the field dejected. Sam glared at Fawad with a murderous look on his face. Fawad foresaw what was coming and ran down the corridor with Sam hot at his heels. Indian superstitions, particularly the ones related to cricket, have a habit of coming true at exactly the wrong moments.

Long story short, India lost that match too, and everyone from cricket experts on TV to Velan lambasted them. The newspapers carried opinions from all and sundry on how to rectify the current situation. Amazingly, everyone seemed convinced that Sachin's time was over. They wanted him to retire and make way for new blood –as if Sachin alone was the sole reason for the team's debacle and getting rid of him would solve everything! These people didn't understand the value of Sachin Tendulkar and what he meant to the Indian team. *Surely Sachin was smart enough not to listen to these fools,* thought Sam.

The Kids' Council

"Fawad, do you think Sachin should retire before the World cup?" asked Sam one day during lunch hour.

"Yes!" said Fawad and punched the air, having successfully demolished ten aliens on Sam's Ben10 video game.

"What?" Sam couldn't believe his ears.

"Er…no! Sorry, repeat the question please," said Fawad after he was back in the real world.

"Do you ever listen to what I say?" asked Sam exasperated.

"I do listen to you. I just don't pay attention. Ammi says I have attention deficit disorder." Fawad's chest swelled with pride at having such a magnificent-sounding illness.

Ammi sure was right about that, thought Sam. "You know, I have a brilliant cure for that one. I will show you," said Sam before giving Fawad a knock on the head.

"Ouch! Okay, okay, I get it. No need to get physical," said Fawad, rubbing his head.

Fawad too didn't want Sachin to retire now. One, because he was Sachin and should thus never retire. And second, because he had a running bet with Raju for five 5-stars that Sachin would make his 100th century at the World cup.

"So you actually wanted him to get out the other day? That's why you got up from your seat," said Sam with a look of suspicion.

Fawad side-stepped the question. "That's not important. What's important is that Sachin is way too smart to pay any attention to these silly accusations. He has to play at the World cup, for India's sake," said Fawad before adding, "Also for the sake of my five 5-stars."

Although the second reason was pretty silly, Sam was happy with Fawad's views. Even a kid could see how important it was for Sachin to play at the World Cup.

****

It seemed that Sachin didn't share Sam and Fawad's optimism on his chances of playing at the World cup. Sam was not yet up in the morning when Fawad burst into his room, the whole load of the day's newspapers in his hand.

"Sam, Sam, get up!" Fawad was frantically pulling off the blanket. "Looks like we were wrong. Sachin is actually planning to retire now."

All Sam's residual sleep went up in smoke as he caught a glimpse of the headlines. Sachin had returned from the tour midway, citing injury and a need for rest. More importantly, he had called for a press conference in Mumbai, sometime next week. Though the agenda was not mentioned, everyone seemed to be speculating that he would announce his retirement. *Sachin was not that smart after all,* thought Sam dejectedly.

Later in the day, all the news channels – from NDTV to BBC – brought in an array of cricketing experts. They sipped coffee all day and discussed at length the pros and cons of Sachin's retirement. Some even suggested new and innovative ideas on what he could do post-retirement. Even if the guy had no immediate plans of retiring, with all this nonsense, all of them would drive him to do so.

****

"We have to do something about this. We can't let this happen," said Sam at the emergency meeting of the kids' council called in that afternoon.

"What Sam says is true. Clearly, Sachin is not thinking straight and we need to make him do so," echoed Raju, even though he stood to gain in the 5-star bet with Fawad.

"We will write a letter to Sachin asking him not to retire. We all will sign the letter and send it to him tomorrow itself," Sam proposed feverishly.

Everyone nodded in agreement; everyone except Fawad. "A letter is a fine idea. But the guy must receive hundreds of letters each day. There is, realistically speaking, only a slim chance that the he will actually read our letter."

"So what do you suggest," asked Sam.

"We should deliver the letter to him directly. We should go to Mumbai and meet him and convince him to keep on playing, at least till the World cup," said Fawad.

"That is, by far, the most ridiculous idea you have come up with. How can we, small kids, get to Mumbai when we are not even allowed to go outside this hospital? And how are we to meet Sachin even if we get there? No way ...the letter is our best option for now. We should get to work on it immediately." said Sam and dismissed the meeting.

****

Later in the day, Fawad was just getting out of the loo when Sam caught hold of him and pushed him back in.

"Sam, I just came in from there. Nothing much to *download* now," said Fawad and started to get out but was held back by Sam.

"I need to talk to you...in secret." Sam's voice was down to a whisper.

"What for? To listen to some more of my ridiculous ideas," Fawad was still pissed off at his suggestion being dumped so unceremoniously by Sam at the meeting.

"Not ridiculous my friend, but a genius idea," Sam said with a grin.

"What! But you just said there..." said Fawad, confused.

Sam explained, "Fawad, your suggestion is brilliant. No way is Sachin going to read that letter unless we deliver it to him in person. But it will be impossible for all of us to go. So, only you and I will be going to Mumbai. Neither our families nor the doctors here will allow us to leave this hospital. So this thing has to be kept secret from everyone, including the other kids. That's why I shot down your idea at the meeting."

"Oh, so we will escape from here, get to Mumbai and see Sachin. Yippee!" Fawad was bursting with excitement.

"Shh…quiet. The secret won't last long if your keep shouting like this" said Sam.

"Boy, this sounds like a real life adventure. We have got to go soon though. Before Sachin's press meet. Also, secrets aren't exactly my forte," said Fawad while looking sheepish.

"It's fixed then. We will go to Mumbai. We will have to work out the details though. Until then, not a word to anyone. Good night," said Sam as he opened the bathroom door and walked back to his room.

And that's how the journey that would change their lives, Sachin's career and Indian cricket history was planned -in the bathroom of a palliative care centre.

****

The Plan

With their escapade decided upon, Sam and Fawad had a hectic day ahead; so the task of writing the letter was delegated to the others, who set about it in earnest. Meanwhile, Sam had to arrange for the most important thing of all, money.

Sam was ready when dad walked into his room a few hours later. "Hi, dad. I need a thousand rupees."

"Why? What for?"His father was surprised by this sudden request.

"It is Fawad's birthday next week and all of us are planning a surprise party for him," Sam lied.

Mr. Martin had never denied his son anything. He wasn't going to start now. He took out his wallet and gave the money to Sam. Sam managed to catch a glimpse of the stack of ATM cards in the wallet and a sudden idea struck him.

"Dad, let me see my photo in that wallet," he said and snatched the wallet away before his father could say anything. His mobile rang at the same moment and Mr. Martin was soon involved in an animated conversation with the person at the other end of the line. Fortune favors the brave, thought

Sam as he deftly plucked one card from the stack and hid it under his pillow.

After Dad left, Sam grabbed the money and the ATM card and dashed to Fawad's room.

"Did you get it?" Fawad asked anxiously.

"Sure did," said Sam as he flashed the thousand-rupee bill. "I also got us some insurance money, in case of an emergency," he said and showed Fawad the ATM card.

"What are you going to do with it? You need a password for that," said Fawad skeptically.

"I have seen dad use it countless times. Sometimes he let me punch in the password. He is good at a lot of things but remembering passwords in not exactly his strong point, so all his cards have either mine or Tony's birthdays as passwords. By the way, if dad asks, your birthday is next week."

"That's okay. Don't let him meet Senthil uncle though. He thinks my birthday was last month," said Fawad with a conspiratorial air.

"What did you lie to Doctor Uncle for?" asked Sam.

"For this," Fawad pulled out a box of chocolates from his backpack. "In fact, I have a birthday for each month I have been here. It takes a bit of planning but for a genius like me it is very easy. Though you have to make sure that the nurse aunties' schedules are different."

Fawad sure was a genius, though of a twisted kind, thought Sam as he munched on a goody from the chocolate box.

"I have our backpacks ready as per your instructions," Fawad said as he pulled out two bags from under his bed.

Sam examined the bags. His bag was filled with all the items that he had asked for, mostly clothes, toiletries and other essentials. The other bag (Fawad's) didn't exactly fit Sam's "as per instructions". It was stuffed with a toothbrush, a bottle of water and loads of chocolates. When Sam looked at him questioningly, Fawad's one-line explanation was "food."

Next on the agenda was to chart a course for their journey. They had already decided that the best way to get out of the hospital was during visiting hours when the place was chock-a-block with people. Dressed in street clothes they could blend with the crowd and get past the poor, sleepy man who served as security. Their bald heads would draw some attention but Fawad had thought of that and arranged for two baseball-style caps. So, with a little bit of luck, getting past the walls of this hospital wouldn't be a problem at all. What to do once outside was the real problem. The Internet was the solution. Off to the systems guy in the administrative wing they went.

"Jaleel uncle, how are you today?" Fawad began sweet-talking from the get go. The guy knew everyone in this hospital.

"Why, Fawad, I am fine. What are you doing here?" Jaleel looked up from the computer screen and appeared to be glad to see a human face for a change.

"Oh nothing, just roaming around. Haven't seen you around lately..." Fawad continued with this agenda.

"Yeah, I caught the flu and was bedridden for a couple of days. You are like the exclusive news reporter of this hospital."

"No, no, I just happened to hear Jameela sister over at the canteen. She was asking about you. She sounded concerned..." Fawad left the bait dangling in midair.

In two seconds, Jaleel's cheeks had taken on a strawberry milkshake color. *Guys,* thought Sam as Jaleel made some lame excuses for a coffee break and went practically sprinting in the direction of the canteen.

"Well, he sure got rid of the flu," said Fawad before adding, "but he's about to catch something much worse."

"How do you know all these things," Sam asked, amazed.

"I am the Sherlock Holmes of India. I have eyes everywhere," Fawad said. He was already on the computer.

"Let's try Google maps first," said Sam and joined him.

Over the next 10 minutes, they plotted the way from the hospital to the railway station. A train left at around six thirty in the evening, which would take them to Kalyan station by the afternoon of the next day. They also managed to find Sachin's residence and the directions to his place from Kalyan. It seemed simple enough. If all went well, they could meet him and be back here the following evening.

"Hey, check this out ...Sachin's blog," Fawad called out to Sam, who was busy taking printouts of everything.

Sam took one look at the screen and was devastated. It was only two lines. *"It has been along and eventful journey. But I* *am tired now. Maybe it's time to…,"*Sachin's unfinished line did say a lot.

"We need to get there soon ... before he does something in haste," Sam said as he folded up the printouts and pushed them beneath his shirt. Just in time … as Jaleel returned from the canteen with a wide grin plastered across his face.

"What are you kids still doing here?" Jaleel

"Nothing … we were just guarding your computer. Plus, checking out some new video games while at it," Fawad said before immediately changing the topic. "Anyway, how did it go with Jameela sister?"

The strawberry color returned; clearly, some success was had there. Suddenly, it dawned on Jaleel that discussing his love interest with a bunch of twelve-year olds was absurd. So he shoo'd them away and went back to his desk. With Jameela sister and his future with her occupying most of his mind, Jaleel didn't pay much attention to the Google maps of Mumbai and IRCTC sites opened up on his computer.

****

The Escape

The first part of their plan worked out beautifully –thanks to a stroke of genius from Sam. They were ready with their backpacks and caps, dressed in T-shirts and shorts. With the visiting hours almost over, their families had already left. Sam and Fawad mingled in with the outgoing crowd and were almost at the gate when they realized that the mob was not enough cover from the security guy. They slipped back and had almost made up their minds to try again the next day.

Just then Sam saw the phone lying unguarded at the empty reception desk. He made his way to the phone while Fawad kept watch. The extensions for the various phones on the premises were listed there. He dialed the one for the security booth at the entrance gate and waited.

"Hello, Security," a sleepy voice answered.

"The Chief is asking for you. Meet him immediately in his office." Sam put in some bass in his voice and had managed to sound stern.

Poor Chandran trembled with anticipation. The only other time he had been to the Chief's office was when he had been appointed four years ago. Now suddenly he had been summoned again. Somebody must have complained. He shouldn't have drunk so much last night. What was he going to say? Better to deny the whole thing. All this and much more was rattling around in his mind as Chandran called the manager's office and asked for a temporary replacement at the entrance. However he was so pre-occupied that he was already on his way to the chief's room before the replacement guard showed up. Sam and Fawad grabbed the opportunity and coolly made their way outside the hospital as poor Chandran sat outside the Chief's office contemplating alternate career options.

****

The auto rickshaw stand outside the hospital's entrance was jam-packed with people haggling with the auto drivers. The drivers knew a business opportunity when they saw one and ceremoniously showed up every day only during the visiting hours.

"Where to?" the driver asked as Sam and Fawad got into the first auto in line.

"Calicut Railway station," said Sam.

"Where are you two kids running off to?" asked the auto driver as he turned back to look at his fare and found that two children had plonked themselves on his back seat.

"We are going to Mumbai," Fawad blurted out as Sam's heart skipped a beat. However, Fawad didn't stop there. "To act in a movie. We have been offered a role with Shahrukh in his next science flick," Fawad rambled on while Sam kept tugging at his shirt to stop.

"Yeah, right! And I am Hrithik driving around in an auto to get into the skin of the character for my next movie," the auto guy said, dismissing Fawad's delusional idea with a wave as he fired up his engine.

"You sure look like Hrithik. Maybe we can get you a role if you come with us," said Fawad the master of *maskagiri*.

"If Shahrukh's last sci-fi was any indication of this next movie, then I am better off driving an auto," said the auto guy as he slowly picked up speed.

Sam heaved a sigh of relief as they drove out of the medical college campus. The palliative care building slowly disappeared from view as the auto made its way to their destination. He turned to Fawad and gave him a stern look for almost spoiling it with his chatter box.

"What! I know what I am doing," said Fawad defensively. "Sometimes, people dismiss the truth even if you proclaim it from rooftops. Particularly if the truth is of the absurd kind," whispered Fawad.

"Let's sit back and enjoy the ride. It will be our last auto ride once Dad and Mom get to know about it." Sam said and closed his eyes.

They did enjoy the ride. It was their first view of the outside world in months. The view didn't last for much though. The auto guy appeared to transform into Schumacher incarnate once he reached the highway. As his F1 auto twisted and turned through the traffic, the simple auto ride became more of a Disney roller coaster. It was a pity it lasted only 15 minutes.

****

Having duly paid the auto, they were about to enter the railway station when Sam noticed the ATM kiosk nearby. Better keep some money on hand than go searching for an ATM throughout their sojourn, thought Sam. Handing the rest of his money to Fawad, he asked him to get the tickets while Sam made his way to the ATM.

The ticket guy was surprised to look up and see only a tiny hand reaching over the counter. It was accompanied by a squeaky voice coming from somewhere below, "Two tickets to Mumbai." He reached over and saw Fawad's eager eyes staring up at him.

"Who are you with, boy?" the ticket guy was suspicious.

"My dad. He's at the ATM counter over there. Asked me to stand in line for the tickets," said Fawad understanding the guy's intentions and lying promptly.

With a lie already in place, why not stretch it further thought Fawad as he built on the theme, "Dad has business in Mumbai. We go there very often. Usually we stay with uncle Bilal there. Nice guy. Always takes me out to Juhu beach every evening we are there. Nice ice-*golas* they make there ... lots of colors and flavors. My favorite one though..."

"Okay, Okay, fine. I don't need to hear about ice-golas right now." The ticket guy grew impatient as he saw the huge line building up behind Fawad. "What class?"

"Five B," Fawad replied.

"What! There is no such class," the guy shot back.

"There is," Fawad was not about to give up on the only truth he had uttered all day, "Five B, Bharti Vidya Mandir. I will move to sixth class in a few months though."

"Not the class you study kid, the train's class!" The ticket guy's patience was running short.

"Trains have class too ... where do they study?" said Fawad toying with the already frustrated guy.

No point in wasting time with this kid. Better to get rid of him as soon as possible, thought the ticket guy. He handed Fawad the tickets for general class.

Fawad was nowhere to be seen near the ticket counter when Sam came back from the ATM. As he looked around, an ice cream cone was stuck under his nose from behind, "Eat, drink and be merry, my boy ... for tomorrow we may run out of ice creams," Fawad said. He had two more cones in his other hand.

"You continue in this fashion and surely that will happen very soon," said Sam before coming back to the topic at hand, "Did you get the tickets?"

Sure did ... if anyone asks, you are my Dad," Fawad said as he handed the tickets to Sam.

"It definitely looks so," said Sam as he plucked the ticket from Fawad's hand. "How much money we got left?"

"About 400. We will need more than that if we want to come back. Or else we can try ticketless travel and hope for the best."

"There won't be a need for that. I took out another five thousand rupees from the ATM." Sam flashed the money at Fawad whose eyes lit up at the sight in front of him.

"Boy! We can live like kings with that kind of money. When we are done with our primary agenda, we will roam Mumbai. We could hire a car and go to Juhu, visit all the stadiums, see all the movie stars... and, and... maybe we should stay at the Taj..." Fawad was at a loss for words.

"Whoa easy now. Let's concentrate on the task at hand and get to Mumbai first," Sam said as they heard the train coming.

As the Mangla express came to a halt, Sam was cooking up strategies to corner Sachin for a talk. Fawad was already at the *chowpati* enjoying spicy *chaat* and slurping up multi-colored ice-golas.

****

Mumbai

Mumbai was crowded. That was Sam's first impression as he stepped out onto the platform. Fawad didn't mind the crowd as much as the mad rush of the people. He never managed to step on the platform; a mob literally carried him away on its shoulders right up to the exit. Both of them were however relieved to get off the train.

The general compartment of any train in India is not a very nice place, especially for two sick kids. In the train, jam-packed with passengers of all sizes, Sam and Fawad had spent most of the journey cramped up near the doorway. The stifling heat, constant pushing and shoving and, of course, that magical smell of an Indian railways toilet all combined forces to make life unbearable. More than once, they considered getting off and turning back. But they persisted and were soon rewarded with seats on a top bunk.

Their happiness was short lived. As night fell, the guy seated next to them who, till then seemed a decent enough human being, turned into a snoring machine. The amazing cacophony of weird noises produced by him ensured that the boys never got any sleep. Sometime during the night, the snoring machine was replaced by a bawling child whose screams were ultrasonic. The net effect, as far as Sam and Fawad were concerned, was the same – a sleepless and miserable journey.

A big line of taxis waited outside the station. Sam and Fawad made their way to the nearest one and were about to get in when the driver came running around and shouting at the same time.

"Stop, stop! Where do you think you are going?"

"We have to get to Bandra," said Sam.

The driver took one look at his fare and decided that they were trouble. Two shaggy-looking kids who were apparently travelling alone suggested mostly of credit unworthiness. He was about to offer some lame excuse when suddenly one of the kids pulled out a big wad of cash from his bag.

"We have money, if that's what you are worried about." Sam flashed the money in front of the driver – a mistake.

Now the driver was sure that the kids were trouble. *Definitely thieves. Should get rid of them as soon as possible*. He thought as he looked around and spotted a constable at a *chai* stall on the other side of the road.

"You two wait here. I will just pay for my chai and be back in 2 seconds," the driver said and ran off towards the stall.

"*Salaam sahib*!" The driver greeted the constable who was busy stuffing his face with *vada-paav*.

"What is it?" said the constable looking up from his plate. "Oh, Ramakant! Come sit. Sorry, I can't join you people for *teenpatti*. I am on duty now."

"Sure, I can see that," Ramakant observed dryly as another paav vanished down the hatch. "That's not what I am here for. There are two street kids there by my taxi. Thieves with bags stuffed with money."

"Is it? Let's get those buggers," said the constable and immediately sprang into action. Food wastage is a crime in a country like India, where half the population never gets any. So he dutifully polished off the last traces of food on his plate before springing into action for a second time. With brisk steps, he made his way to the taxi stand; the driver followed suit.

"Sahib, when you catch those thieves you will get a medal, right? Maybe, there should be a small reward for me too, in that case," the driver said expectantly.

"You will get your reward when you show me the thieves. Now, where are they?"

"Right here," the driver said as he pointed towards his taxi and saw a dirty mongrel curled up on the spot where the two kids had been.

The boys had vanished –along with his reward and constable sahib's medal.

****

The boys were in fact on their way to Bandra on a city bus.

It was Fawad who had spotted the driver talking to the policeman and immediately smelled trouble. A quick scan of the surroundings revealed a small alley a few yards away and he quickly made for it dragging Sam behind him. Once there, they observed quietly as the taxi driver was blasted by the policeman for wasting his time. He warned the driver against drinking during duty time and was back at his seat by the chai shop within a second. As the driver moped around his taxi, Sam spotted a bus coming in from a distance. They jumped into it as it stopped and were soon on the way to their destination.

"Phew! Our adventure was almost over there," Sam exclaimed as he plonked himself on a vacant seat. Fawad sat next to him as the bus sped away on the crowded roads of Mumbai.

"Not really," said Fawad, "The adventure would have taken a different turn though. Police station, jail and then torture.

"Watching all those Hindi movies has turned your brains to mush. We are not underworld thugs or terrorists," Sam chided Fawad.

"A good enough beating and you will agree to being anything, thug or terrorist. Hell, they can make you confess to being Osama," said Fawad. As an afterthought, he added, "A less hairy version of him at least."

Sam was about to whack Fawad with his bag when the conductor suddenly materialized in front of them.

"Tickets."

"Two tickets to Bandra," said Fawad as he handed over the money.

"This bus goes only till Chinchpokli. Get down there and catch the No.17 to Bandra," the conductor announced rapidly and was off before either of the boys could react.

"Did you understand that?" Sam asked Fawad.

"Nope, flew right over my bald head. Don't worry though. We have made it this far. We will get to our man somehow. Relax and enjoy the ride." Fawad opened up his bag and brought out two chocolate bars.

Mumbai and its people flew past their window as the boys sat happily munching on their treats, nursing dreams of meeting with Sachin. They were so close…

****

Away for the Weekend

A few changes of buses and a couple of wrong routes later, the boys finally ended up in Bandra. By this time, they had slept off most of the fatigue of their train journey and were full of energy thanks to a couple of chocolate bars each.

"Excuse me, sir", Fawad said to an old man standing at the bus stop, "Can you tell us where Sachin Tendulkar's house is?"

The old man was busy talking on his phone and simply pointed his finger vaguely in some direction. Sam and Fawad made their way in that direction. A milkman coming along on his cycle and a fat lady hurrying along with her kid also reacted in the same manner. The direction they all pointed to was the same, so the boys were assured that they were on the right track.

"It seems people here are not very much into talking," Sam observed.

"You have me to talk to. Anytime, anywhere, anything," Fawad chirped. The bounce was back in his feet. The exertion of travel had drained the color off his face and he had also been running a slight fever. However, the thrill of meeting

Sachin, and the added incentive of roaming around Mumbai had lifted his spirits. The downside was that his non-stop babbling was also back.

"I do like to talk to someone with brains from time to time," Sam said, mocking Fawad.

"That's right. Hence, I am the best choice you have." Fawad, of course, totally missed the mocking part. "Make hay while the sun shines," Fawad added as an afterthought. He had this habit of pushing unsuitable proverbs into totally unrelated issues.

"What?" Sam's flabbergasted expression said it all.

"You know, it's almost noon. So the sun is shining and we should probably start making some hay with Sachin," said Fawad unconvincingly. Only he understood the meaning of this.

"It would be better if I talk to Sachin while you keep your mouth shut. Better still, you should probably play outside with his dog while we talk," Sam suggested.

"I don't think he has a dog ...never seen him with one." Fawad wouldn't give up so easily.

"When have you seen Sachin in person?" asked Sam.

"Oh, I haven't seen him in person. But countless times I have seen him playing cricket on TV, also in a lot of ads. Never once was he seen with a dog," Fawad said with utmost sincerity.

"You should get your head checked. How will Sachin drag his dog onto a cricket field? Or into a TV commercial?" Sam was at the point of losing his cool.

Fawad realized this and riled him up some more, "You are right. You know, sometimes you do talk some sense in between loads of nonsense."

The next second Fawad realized that Sam was hurling something at him. He ducked smartly and was off in a flash with Sam hot on his heels.

****

They both stared in awe at the massive gate in front of them. Beyond it lay manicured lawns and a huge white bungalow. Something else lay inside those gates –the person they were here to meet. "Sachin Ramesh Tendulkar," announced the golden plaque at the gate. As soon as they advanced towards the gates, a uniformed guy materialized out of the security booth that they hadn't noticed until now. A huge man with a Veerappan-style moustache and a perpetual scowl on face, Murugan was used to gate crashers and crazy fans of all kinds that turned up every now and then. Not one had been able to get past him until now – a fact of which he was proud. These two kids were however, different.

"You can't barge into anyone's house like this, leave alone Sachin *sahib's,*" Murugan announced with an air of authority.

"It is very important that we meet Sachin. Please allow us to go through," Sam pleaded with the guy.

"Not possible. Even bigwigs wait patiently at this gate to meet my sahib. No one can harm him while I am still alive," Murugan said and thumped his chest with pride.

"What? Why would we want to harm him? We are just kids," Sam said while looking pleadingly at the guy.

"No one can meet him without an appointment," Murugan clarified.

Fawad, who was quiet till now, suddenly burst in on the conversation, "But we do have an appointment. We are kids from the Children's Cancer Foundation, scheduled to meet Sachin regarding a promotional campaign."

"But I do not have you on my list here," said Murugan.

"Must be some mistake there. The meeting was scheduled for tomorrow but Sachin sir himself called us and asked us to meet him here today. He may have forgotten to tell you that," the lies kept flowing from Fawad's mouth.

"Even so, not on the list means not fit to enter." Murugan was adamant.

Suddenly Fawad dropped to the ground in a heap with his half- closed eyes staring blankly into space. Murugan looked on with concern as Sam bundled up Fawad in his arms.

"Please get him some water, immediately," Sam said, frantic and on the verge of tears.

Murugan had turned to stone for a second; but his ears registered the command and he dashed into his cabin and back in the blink of an eye. He gave the bottle of water to Sam.

A few splashes of water and a few gulps later, Fawad groggily opened his eyes. "Must be the heat and exhaustion from the travel," he said as he sat up, still looking dazed.

"What is wrong with you, my boy? Should I call for an ambulance?" Murugan was now at his helpful best.

"He has cancer … in fact, both of us do," Sam replied curtly.

"It is my last wish to see Sachin in person. We have come a long way for that purpose. However, it looks like my dream will remain unfulfilled because of a heartless gatekeeper," sighed Fawad.

Ashamed and ridden with guilt, Murugan kept mum for some time. Then he took the boys into his cabin and ran back into the house. He came back a few minutes later with two glasses of fresh juice.

"Please have this and forgive me for my behavior. I didn't realize that you kids were sick," Murugan said.

"It's okay. We just want to meet your master. It is very important that we do so immediately," Sam said as he sipped on his glass of juice.

"But Sachin sir is away on a holiday. He will be back only on Monday, that is, two days from now. Just come back then and I will make sure that you get to see him," said Murugan; he was at his helpful best now.

Murugan's helpful best was however not enough for the boys. His words had dashed their dream of meeting their hero today. Uncertainty loomed as Sam and Fawad made their way back from Sachin's house, dejected at the turn of events.

****

Well, there go our hopes of a quick rendezvous and back home in a jiffy, thought Sam as they stood at the bus-stop.

"How are you feeling now?" Sam asked Fawad as they reached the bus stop.

"I am fine. What could be wrong with me?"Fawad asked.

"In case you forgot, you fainted there," Sam said, slightly irritated.

"Oh, that was just an act to get our path cleared. Proved to be useless, however," Fawad replied with a mischievous grin on his face.

Sam whacked Fawad on the back of his head with his bag. "You idiot. I was worried sick back there. Almost thought you were a goner. You should give me a signal when you are up to such things."

"Relax, man … and sorry for that. It did help us though. We are friends with Sachin's gatekeeper now," Fawad said.

"How is that going to help us? Sachin won't be back for another two days and we can't stay here for that long." Sam was dejected.

"Oh yes we can. We came this far to meet him and we are not going back until we do so." Fawad was confidence personified.

"But how will we survive? We don't know anyone here. We don't have a place to stay and …

Fawad cut in, "We will manage somehow. We have money which will help. I still have my health and good looks. Plus we can always play the cancer trump card, if needed."

"Your health and good looks?" Sam repeated incredulously before adding, "Though you are delusional, you also are an eternal optimist. A delusional optimist, very rare species."

"Fine, fine, you can praise me later. Let's do the most important thing first," Fawad said as he pointed towards the road.

"What important..." Sam couldn't complete his sentence because a bus was making its way to the stop. Sam looked up to see Fawad pointing at its board, which proclaimed its destination in bold red letters: JUHU.

****

Sun, Sand and Thieves

The little boy had been staring at Sam and Fawad for quite some time now. Sam was aware of this and had ignored it initially. But it was gradually turning into a nuisance. He quietly whispered into Fawad's ears, "We should do something about that boy."

"What boy?" Fawad had been in ice-gola heaven and was oblivious to all worldly matters, let alone a pesky kid.

They were at the Juhu beach, along with the rest of the population of Mumbai, as it seemed to Sam. There were only a few people initially when they had landed there in the afternoon hours. But by evening the crowd had steadily built up to its present volume. The fading light brought in hordes of people. Something about sunsets attracted the human mind - something that was clearly beyond the understanding of the boys.

They had spent the better part of the day frolicking in the waters of the Arabian Sea. Though they had beautiful beaches back home, their illness prevented them from enjoying the waters as other kids would. Beach visits were mostly restricted to watching the waves from a distance like oldies.

Here, the illness factor was still there, but no dad and mom to supervise. The gay abandon of youth took over and they rode the waves like there was no tomorrow, which was true in a sense.

Their marine exploits had tired them considerably and so they withdrew to the numerous stalls that lined the beach. It was here, while lapping up ice-golas that Sam had noticed a small kid eyeing them.

"What do you want, boy?" Sam asked with some irritation in his voice.

The boy pointed to the ice-golas they were having. Sam examined the boy more closely and saw his tattered clothes, seriously malnourished appearance and generally unkempt look.

Fawad saw the same too. "Oh, the poor kid is probably hungry. He must be one of the many destitute slum kids here, like in the Slumdog film. Hey Sam, buy one for him too." Fawad was in a magnanimous mood; part of the reason for him making this trip was fulfilled today. Also it is easy to be extravagant when the money is not yours.

Sam was about to protest, but it was useless to argue with Fawad when he was in such a mood. He ordered an ice-gola, paid up with some money from his backpack and handed it over to the boy who smiled as he took the treat and immediately started lapping it up in frenzy.

"See, we have one more good deed in our kitty," said Fawad as they looked at the happy kid.

"With the load of lies that you already have in your bag, you will certainly need many more of these good deeds by the time you meet Allah." Sam chided Fawad.

"Lies... what lies?" Fawad said in mock disbelief as they watched the setting sun together.

Mesmerized by the scenic beauty and the humdrum of the crowd, the boys lost all track of time. "Boy, this is so nice. Good that Sachin went on the break and we got the chance to come here," quipped Fawad.

"We do have to still figure out a place to stay," Sam reminded him.

"That's where the sympathetic gatekeeper comes in," Fawad said. "He will do anything for this sick kid."

Sam was about to protest but realized that Fawad was right. Among this sea of humanity, Sachin's gatekeeper was the only person they actually knew; he was their most promising option. "You are a genius."

"I know, I know. It's in my *jeans*, or rather shorts," Fawad replied nonchalantly.

"Don't go overboard with your genius-ness," Sam said. "Let's get out of here and back to your gatekeeper friend."

They turned around to pick up their belongings and make the journey back to Sachin's house. It took them a moment to soak it in and realize the truth. The boy was gone; more importantly, so was Sam's bag along with all their money.

Disaster...

****

A Starry Night

It was a star-filled sky that Sam and Fawad stared at as they lay there on the beach. Most of the evening crowd had wandered off back to the comfort of their homes. The few street dwellers were getting ready to turn in for the night at their usual spots.

"How are we going to get back without any money?" Sam broke the silence with the most obvious question.

"More importantly, how will we survive here for two days?" Fawad answered with a question of his own.

"You are still thinking of staying back here! As soon as we manage to get some money, we make our way back to our homes. We are neck-deep in trouble as it is, without the additional bother of surviving here."

"Fine, fine … as you say. For the time being, let's find a place to sleep," said Fawad, yawning already.

The two of them walked up and down the beach and finally managed to find an empty bench. The cold breeze coming from the sea was a bother and the boys were shivering as they lay down on the bench. The day's exploits however had tired them so much that they soon dozed off, the cold and damp notwithstanding.

****

The insistent poking in the ribs was getting irksome by the minute; Sam responded in kind with a vicious elbow of his own, right at Fawad's midsection.

"Hey, why did you do that?" asked Fawad, jolted back to the real world from his chocolate dreamland.

"Tit for tat ... you poke, I poke," Sam replied in a sleepy voice.

"What poke? I didn't do anything," protested Fawad before dozing off again.

"Then what ..." Sam stopped mid-sentence as he opened his eyes and saw a small figure staring at them. He jumped upright and took a closer look at the small figure. It was the kid who had stolen his bag!

"You little thief!! It's because of you that we are stuck here. Where's my bag?" shouted Sam as he grabbed the kid by his collar.

Fawad had woken up upon hearing all the commotion. It took him a moment to realize what was happening.

"Come here you little bugger; I will teach you a lesson you will never forget," said Fawad as he too grabbed at the boy.

The boy, who hadn't spoken so far, suddenly began to make frantic gestures with his hands.

"What the hell are you doing? Tell us where our bag is, or else..." Sam said, the threat evident in his tone.

"He can't," said a new voice that emerged from the darkness behind the boy. "He's a mute." A tall lanky fellow of around the same age as the boys emerged from behind the small one.

Sam and Fawad instinctively loosened their grip on the kid. The boy gave them a warm smile and went back to join his big brother.

"His name is Shyam. I am Munna. Pleased to meet you," the big guy said as he extended his hand.

"Sam ... and this is Fawad," the boys shook hands.

"Why did you come back, kid?" Fawad asked the mute one.

"He was following you the whole day. You seemed like the rich kids who wouldn't be bothered much by the loss of a bag. But then, it seems you are homeless ones like us. He's here to return your bag." Munna spoke for Shyam.

"Don't you boys have a home to go to? What are you doing here?" asked Munna.

Munna and Shyam listened quietly as Sam and Fawad narrated the story of their incredible journey. It was nearing dawn by the time they were finished.

Fawad yawned as he finished their tale. "So that's about it. We have to hang on here for one more day. Then we can meet Sachin and head back to our place," he said.

"I am amazed ... both by your daring and your stupidity," exclaimed Munna.

"Well, that's us. He's the stupid one," quipped Fawad pointing towards Sam and immediately got a slap on the wrist in reply.

"What are you planning to do today? You can't hang around here the whole day. The *policewallahs* will be out with their *lathis* very soon to drive away people like us," said Munna.

"We were hoping to get back to Sachin's house and try our luck with the watchman there. He's a close friend of Fawad's," said Sam winking at Fawad.

"What if the guy is not there? They do work in shifts. You know that, right?" asked Munna.

"Well, in that case, we will be pretty much out of options." Sam began to be worried as the reality of what Munna said struck him.

"We can always try our luck at the Taj," suggested Fawad.

"Yeah, right! They sure will allow two kids to check in by themselves," Munna said, his words dripping with sarcasm.

"He's right. No hotel, let alone the Taj, will lend us a room. On the contrary, they may try to hand us over to the police guys, like that Taxi driver did," Sam said with some concern. Trying their luck with hotels and such was out of question.

"Such a huge city, big *metropolitician* and all. So many buildings and stuff, but no place for two kids to stay. No wonder they didn't make this the capital of India," said Fawad, apparently furious.

Sam wanted to correct Fawad's 'metropolitician' error. He also was not sure if the lack of living space for two on-the-run kids was the reason for Mumbai losing out in the race to become a capital city. But he thought it prudent to keep his trap shut when Fawad was in such a mood. Also, Fawad was still ranting.

"Boy, it all seemed so easy when we planned this thing out. Reach Mumbai, meet Sachin and go back. It seems we didn't think about this aspect of our trip in much detail," Fawad said, stating the obvious.

"You talk of meeting Sachin as if he was some low- life like me who wanders around on the beach and you could run into him just like that. You guys sure are more stupid that I first gave you credit for," commented Munna.

Sam ignored Munna's taunts, "Let's take this one at a time. Our first concern is to find a place to stay for today. What do we do about that?"

Shyam, who till now was listening to all of them go at each other, suddenly jumped into the fray. After some animated gesturing between him and Munna, he grabbed both Sam and Fawad by their arms and smiled at them.

"He wants you to come with us back to our place," was the only thing Munna said as he started walking away. Sam and Fawad looked at each other and then at Shyam. The boy was insistent and neither of them could think of anything better. *One problem solved,* they thought as they followed Munna and Shyam back to their place ...

****

Home Sweet Home

"This is your place?" Sam asked with some concern.

"Yep! Home, sweet home," Munna said as he proudly presented them with a view of a huge water pipe. Sam and Fawad had no idea where exactly they were but from the looks of it, it seemed like a huge garbage dump. The place looked completely desolate except for piles of rubbish and a whole stack of those pipes, supposedly for a new pipeline coming up in the near future.

"But how can you live here? More importantly, how can we live here?" Fawad said, a disgusted look upon his face."Oh, this is only a temporary setup. You see, we are building a ten-storey villa and will be moving into it shortly." Sarcasm shone through in Munna's words.

"Well, something's better than nothing," said Sam as he dumped his bag into the pipe.

"Doesn't the smell bother you?" Fawad was still skeptical.

"You will get used to it in a day or two. Anyway, we are out for work during the major part of the day. And at night, we don't sleep here. Too many dogs around."

"So where do you sleep?" asked Sam

"In an under-construction apartment out there," Munna said and pointed in the general direction of the city.

"Why can't we go there now? At least we can be rid of this horrible smell," Fawad said as he tried to cover his face with a handkerchief from his bag.

"Because it is under construction, idiot. During the day, people work there. At night, we slip in through the barricades and then we own the building."

"What happens when they are finished with the building?" asked Fawad.

"Then we move to another construction site. It's a big city. Some new building is always coming up somewhere," said Munna. "We are like nomads. This is our only permanent abode."

"Why is that? They will move these pipes when they start laying the pipeline," said Sam.

"These pipes have been here for as long as I can remember. Thanks to the speed and efficiency of our government, they will remain so for another decade or so."

"What exactly did you mean by work earlier?" asked Sam.

"We are handymen. We do all kinds of jobs. Mostly, however, we specialize in what Shyam here did to you."

Shyam had been rummaging through a pile of assorted things kept at one end of the pipe. He looked up with a sheepish grin on his face and then ducked back into his pile. A minute later, he materialized with a chocolate bar in hand that he duly handed over to Fawad.

"Oh, No, no!! We can't hog your food," Fawad said as he tried to hand the thing back to Shyam. Shyam, however, would have none of it; he backed off while gesturing for Sam and Fawad to have a go at the chocolate.

"Tell you what, we can all have one," said Fawad as he pulled out more chocolate from the stockpile in his bag.

As the boys sat around munching on their goodies, more inmates of the pipe-house started to show up. Around half a dozen of them gathered around them, looking expectantly at the chocolate bars lying around. A round of introductions later, they all sat down and proceeded to ransack Fawad's bag. Once the last of the wrappers had been licked clean, the rest of the boys wandered off while Sam and Fawad changed into a fresh pair of clothes.

"I won't be needing this anymore," said Fawad as he tossed aside his now empty bag.

"I am still hungry. Let's go and have a decent breakfast at some place nice,"suggested Sam.

In reply, Shyam pulled out his empty pockets while Munna flashed a thumbs-down sign.

"That's not a problem at all. Sam here has tons of money," said Fawad.

"It's not exactly tons of money. But we can manage a nice meal. Let's go." Sam was already out in the open.

****

Rahim's *dhaba* couldn't exactly be described as the nicest hangout in town but Sam and Fawad were relieved to be away from the smelly pipe-home. The food was more than decent as could be deduced from the glee on Shyam and Munna's faces. The spread in front of them was a far cry from the stale bread and other leftovers that they were used to.

"That sure did hit the spot," said Munna as he wiped his plate clean.

"That's our first real meal in almost two days," said Fawad as he too polished off the last remaining crumbs.

"Two days! That's our first real meal in as long as I can remember. Thank you for this," said Munna. Shyam too silently mouthed the words.

Sam felt sorry for the two of them. He and Fawad had never had to worry about their next meal; they had never had to work to make a living. Compared to Shyam and Munna, for whom each day was a new struggle, their life was heaven. He decided to give them a slice of that heaven during the time he was with them. One look at Fawad and he understood that he too was thinking much along the same lines.

"You know what, why don't we spend the day having fun?" suggested Sam.

"Means what?" asked Munna.

"We will be here only for another day at the most and probably will not get another chance to see Mumbai again.

Why don't you show us around given our limited knowledge of this city," Sam clarified.

"But we have to go to work. We are already pretty late..." Munna started to protest but was cut short by Fawad.

"Oh, you can give the poor people of Mumbai a rest for the day. Let them roam free without constantly checking their pockets."

"But..." Munna was still reluctant and looked towards Shyam. Shyam gave a thumbs-up sign, which cleared away any remaining doubts in his mind. "Fine, let's get to it then," he said and stood up.

"Where do we begin?" asked Fawad.

"The place you were originally planning to stay at – the Taj," replied Munna with a nonchalant air.

****

The Taj was huge alright and the Gateway of India was also pretty nice. But what grabbed Sam and Fawad's attention was the pigeons.

"Why do all of them keep hanging around? Don't they have better things to do?" asked Fawad.

"Oh, no, no. They are only seen here on weekends. Today is Sunday,*na* ... no work. The rest of the days the adults go to office while the kids go to school." Munna was dead serious.

Sam burst out laughing; Fawad's bulb took an extra second to light up. "Good one. So you do have a sense of humor."

"Shyam and I used to be based here. We used to see these birds daily. That was before some idiots attacked the Taj there and killed lots of people. Thereafter the police drove away all of us."

"You could have come back later. There are lots of beggars hanging around here now," said Sam.

"Yeah, but the place was completely deserted for days afterwards. Also, the beach provided much easier pickings, particularly with bozos like you showing up every now and then." Munna's comment drew a short jab from Sam and the two of them proceeded to engage in a mock fight.

Meanwhile, Fawad and Shyam were busy with trying to catch one of the pigeons. They tried many of Fawad's so-called surefire tactics. Live baits (flies), dead baits (the flies died after sometime), "gorilla" methods and sneak attacks. The birds, however, had seen all this and much more during their time here. Not only did they avoid all of Fawad's tricks, they also managed to reward him and Shyam with some birdshit for their efforts.

"Hey, little one," Fawad struggled to catch his breath, "Better we leave these pigeons alone. They are not worth the trouble. We can use regular mail anyway, much safer and easier."

As they walked back towards their friends, Fawad also gestured Shyam to be mum about their failure to Sam. This was totally unnecessary given that the kid was mum anyway.

"So what were you two up to?" Sam asked as Fawad and Munna approached. The question was superfluous as he had seen their unsuccessful hunting expedition.

"Nothing, we were just feeding the birds," Fawad lied.

"Yeah. That we can see," said Munna as he pointed to the gifts from the birds splashed over their shirts, before adding, "We saw your futile attempts, you know."

"It's not our fault, you can't expect "gorilla" warfare to work one-way. The birds were not aware of those tactics, their loss," Fawad said, trying to defend his pride with lame excuses.

"Maybe you should try "gorilla" tactics with Gorillas instead of pigeons," suggested Sam.

"Huh!" Fawad didn't understand anything Sam had just said, "Whatever, I am tired and hungry again. Let's go and have something."

It was afternoon already and Sam was also thinking about lunch. Just then they saw a bike zoom past them with a bright red box attached to it. "Pizza Corner," the bike proclaimed proudly and Sam knew instantly what their lunch would be.

"Where's the nearest Pizza corner?" the question was directed at Munna.

"About two *galis* in that direction," Munna said, "But I don't think they will allow us inside, particularly the 'bird-shit bros' here," he said and pointed to Shyam and Fawad.

"Let's dump them here then, we can have Pizza," said Sam as he started to walk away with Munna in tow.

"I am just joking, you idiots," Sam quickly said as he saw the look on Fawad's face. "We will get you people some decent outfits first. My friends should look at least as smart as I am."

The group then made way for the market place where all of them got new pairs of shirts and trousers. Looking smart in their new outfits, the handsome four made their way to Pizza Corner, where they had a whale of a time. Time flew as they sat gobbling pizzas and chatting away. When they finally left the store, their tummies were full as were their hearts.

The only downside was that Sam had almost run out of all the money. *No problem,* he thought as they returned to their pipe-home, *will withdraw some later from an ATM.* Despite the horrid smell, they were soon sleeping off the exhaustion of their exploits of the day.

****

Face to Face with Sachin

Anuradha had seen a lot of street kids over the past few months. But these kids were somewhat different, smartly dressed and well groomed. Plus the two bald ones seemed out of place in this dump hole. The journalist in her was awakened and she set about trying to clarify things in earnest.

"Hi, kids. I am Anuradha. Can I talk to you guys for some time?" She approached the foursome with a smile.

"Why? What for?" Munna was very hesitant when it came to strangers.

"Well, you see, I am a TV reporter and I am doing a news byte on kids like you," Anuradha said.

"What do you mean by 'kids like us'?" asked Sam.

"She means good looking kids, like me," suggested Fawad. He was probably the only one in the group who took an instant liking to the nice lady.

"Er… not exactly; I meant kids like you who are living off the streets in Mumbai."

"Oh, Ok; Fine," Fawad said with a tinge of disappointment. The instant liking was gone.

Anuradha detected the disappointment and instantly corrected herself, "But you are pretty good looking too. That's why I was drawn to talk to you in the first place."

"OK then ... shoot," said Fawad, the smile back on his face.

"Introductions first. I am Anuradha Solanki, a reporter with NDTV India. Now your turn."

"Munna, Shyam, Fawad," Sam pointed to each of them in turn, "and myself Sam."

"Pleased to meet you all. Now to the main question. How come you all are dressed like that?

"This is how we usually dress, we put the shirts on our torso and shorts over the legs," Munna replied with a smile.

The sarcasm was not lost on Anuradha, "Come on, you know what I mean. You are the most well-dressed street kids I have seen and I have seen quite a few."

Shyam meanwhile was looking expectantly at the lady's bag. Seeing him, she pulled out some goodies from the bag and handed them over to him. He took them, smiled and went back to his place beside Munna.

"You should say thanks when you receive a gift from someone," Anuradha said, trying to give a crash course in etiquette to Shyam.

"He can't," said Sam and Anuradha understood him. She leaned over and mouthed a silent 'sorry' to Shyam before giving him a sympathetic peck on the cheek.

"He can hear though ... pretty well, you know," said Fawad as he saw her silent apology.

Anuradha burst out laughing at her own stupidity. Soon, everyone in the party joined in and just like that, they were friends with the news lady.

****

For the second time in the day, Sam and Fawad narrated their story. At first, Anuradha listened with the interest of a news reporter who smelled an exciting story. By the time they were finished, the news interest waned into the background; she was moved to try and genuinely help these two kids.

"I can help you out. I am supposed to cover Sachin's press meet tomorrow. I can get you two into the conference hall."

"Thanks, but we already have an arrangement there," said Sam as he adjusted his cramping legs in the limited space available. "Barring any unforeseen complications, we will get to meet up with him at his house and convince him to agree with us. If all goes well, there won't be any press meet tomorrow."

"Well, good luck with that then. But if you need my help anytime, just give me a call," Anuradha said as she handed over her card. Fawad reached over and pocketed it.

"Thanks, Anu auntie," said Fawad with a glee. He had this strange hobby of collecting knickknacks, including visiting cards.

"Anu*didi* will do," Anuradha said with a smile. She was, after all, a girl.

"Another thing, when you bring out our story, make me the hero. He can be my side-kick," Fawad said as he pointed to Sam.

"Will someone please kick him," Sam pleaded.

"You are both heroes as far as I am concerned," Anu*didi* intervened to settle the argument. "It's getting late. I should go now. Wish you all the best and hope we meet again," she said while getting up, ready to leave.

The last line was said in all earnestness as she was sure she wanted to meet them again and see how their journey ended.

****

As promised by Munna, their night time abode was a lot better than the pipe home. An under-construction building provided lots of space for running around so that Sam could relieve the cramps from being in the pipe. From the rooftop, it provided a spectacular view of the city. Best of all, it was devoid of the horrid smell.

All this should have provided well for a peaceful and good sleep. But both Sam and Fawad were hyper-excited about the next day, more specifically, about their rendezvous with Sachin. Sleep wasn't on the cards for them; and so they didn't allow the other two boys to sleep either.

"You guys should also come along with us, you know," suggested Sam. "This might be your only opportunity to see Sachin face-to-face."

"And what good will that do? It's not going to change our lives in any way, is it?" Munna said in a dreary voice. He was feeling sleepy.

"You mean that meeting *Sachin* is in no way important to you?" asked Fawad in amazement. The word 'Sachin' was stressed and stretched out to enhance its relevance.

"Look, friend, I don't want to hurt your feelings. But honestly, I don't give a damn whether he retires or plays on ... whether he scores a century or nothing. We have more pressing matters to worry about."

"But..." Fawad was about to protest but Sam took his hand and indicated that he shouldn't. Munna was right; his life was a constant struggle for survival – a life that neither Sam nor Fawad could even begin to comprehend. A life where Sachin or anyone else had no relevance whatsoever.

"Fine, don't meet Sachin then, but you can come to see us off. We will probably leave for our homes once we are done with tomorrow's job," said Sam.

"You mean this is our last night together?" Munna was suddenly sitting upright, the idea of sleep was all gone.

"Yes, by this time tomorrow we will be on a train back home. So enjoy my company while you can," said Fawad.

Shyam got up and gave a warm hug to each of them. The mood had turned slightly melancholic and Sam could see that even Munna's eyes had moistened up.

"Look at that," Fawad suddenly called out, "The tough guy doesn't care about Sachin, but cries when he hears that we are leaving." Fawad had also seen Munna's tears.

"These are tears of joy, you idiot," Munna said as he wiped his eyes.

"Then let me convert them to tears of pain," Sam said and suddenly sprang upon Munna. Fawad and Shyam also joined in and soon they were a big pile of arms and legs rolling about on the floor. The revelry and chit-chat continued long into the night as they made the most of their last few hours together.

****

The day held great promise but began on a pretty bleak note. First, they slept in pretty late, which was a given since their exploits the previous night had dragged on well past midnight. They awoke to the sounds of cement churners and other heavy machinery; the building workers had arrived. Fortunately for the boys, none of the men saw them and they were able to slink past the flimsy barricades.

"Oh no, Anudidi had said that the press meet is at ten-thirty. It's already past eight now." Sam was concerned.

"We can still make it to Sachin's house in time ... if we hurry," Fawad said trying to be optimistic about the situation.

"Not in this traffic. This is peak hour," Munna said, presenting the ground reality.

"Let's try anyway. I have to get some money first. Where's the nearest ATM?" asked Sam.

They sprinted to the nearest ATM, which was around half a kilometer away. And that was when the second hiccup of the day materialized. 'Invalid Card' were the words the ATM screen flashed repeatedly as Sam kept trying in vain. Mr. Martin had discovered that one of his cards was missing and had done the most obvious thing - blocked it. He obviously didn't know then that his own son had taken it. Sam wasn't aware of the developments back home as he stepped away from the ATM counter, dejected.

"Something's wrong with the card ... it won't work," he informed the group.

"Which means what?" asked Fawad.

"This means that we are short on money. There will not be enough for our trip back," Sam said.

"We will worry about getting back later. Let's finish up what we came here for in the first place."

With things back in focus, the foursome hired a taxi, paid upfront to avoid a repeat of their previous experience and asked the driver to step on it. Munna was right about the traffic though and it was close to ten o'clock when they finally reached Sachin's house. And there it was that the third malfunction of the day was waiting in store for them.

"Ah, there you are ... good morning, kids," Murugan called out as he saw Sam and Fawad. "You are in luck. I told Sachin sahib about you two when he reached in the morning. You can meet him when he comes back. Who are your friends?" Murugan enquired of them as he saw Munna and Shyam.

Sam didn't hear the question; neither did he care about it. He was instead caught on the first half of what Murugan had said. "What do you mean 'when he comes back'? He is not here now?" he asked with rising concern.

"He just left for some press meet ... should be back in an hour though. Meanwhile, you can wait here in my room."

"Murugan uncle, we don't have the time to explain everything but it is absolutely necessary that we see Sachin before the press meet," Sam was slightly flustered at this point.

"Sorry, kids. But I can't help you out there," Murugan replied.

"Late again – story of our life for today," Sam said, summing up the situation. Disappointment was writ large on his face.

Murugan felt sorry for the kids, but there was nothing he could do. Munna and Shyam were also clueless and Fawad, for the first time in his life, was out of any ideas.

Suddenly Sam saw a glimmer of hope, "Hey, Fawad, where's that card Anudidi gave you?"

Fawad brightened up as he realized what Sam was thinking. He pulled the card out from his pocket and handed it to Sam.

"Can we use your mobile?" Sam asked Murugan and grabbed at it as he handed it over. Murugan didn't have a clue as to what was going on but the urgency on the kids' faces told him that it was best not to interfere. Sam dialed the number and waited impatiently as it rang.

"Hi, Anudidi, it's Sam from yesterday. Looks like we will be needing your help after all. Please help us get into the press meet. You will be there, na. What's the venue again? Okay, thanks. We will get there as fast as we can."

"Everyone get back in the taxi. We are going to the press meet," Sam said as he jumped in first.

"Murugan uncle, thanks for your help. Can we keep your phone? We may need it. We promise to return it later," said Fawad.

"Sure! Anything to help you kids out. Best of luck," said Murugan as the boys got back in the taxi.

The taxi sped away as Sam gave the venue to the driver. He hoped that Sachin too would run into heavy traffic and prayed for the best.

****

"Has it started?" Sam asked the most relevant question as soon as he spotted Anuradha at the Press Club. They had managed to reach the place in double quick time thanks to some intelligent driving by the driver. He covered much of the distance through hidden alleys and side lanes that were cut off from the main road and its heavy traffic. As a reward, Sam had blindly handed over the rest of his money to the guy. The result: they were totally bankrupt now. But that was not his primary concern at that moment.

"Not yet, he's running a bit late. You are in luck, it seems," said Anuradha. She was happy to see them and, better yet, help them.

"About time we ran into some. Thank you, Anudidi," Fawad said as he panted from the exertion.

"Let's get you into the hall first and then you can thank me," said Anuradha. "I don't think they will allow the whole group to enter though," she added as she looked at the crowd. Counting the four of them, herself and the camera guy, they did make a sizable group.

"It's okay. We will wait here outside," Munna said, suggesting the most plausible option.

"Fine then, why don't you and Shyam wait here in our van while Sam and Fawad come inside with me?" suggested Anuradha and it was decided as such.

"Take off your caps ... it looks suspicious and attracts attention. Let me do the talking at the security booth. If anyone asks, you both are reporters from our kids' channel, here to conduct an exclusive interview with Sachin," she said as she walked hurriedly to the entrance with Sam and Fawad in tow.

All these precautions seemed unnecessary as the guys at the security booth were pretty lenient and easygoing. They took in all the bogus kids' channel and reporter thing from Anuradha; with the number of channels around these days, there sure could be an "NDTV KIDS" one too. Besides, two small children couldn't really be considered much of a security threat. A cursory glance at Anuradha's ID badge and the customary wave of the wand was over in a jiffy and they were whisked into the conference hall. They ran along and managed to grab the nearest possible seats to the dais just as Sachin made his grand entrance.

Phew... face to face with Sachin at last.

****

Mission Accomplished

It's not every day that you get to see your real-life hero in person. They were in front of their hero, Sachin Tendulkar, and for Sam and Fawad, this was it; all their travails were worth it just for this moment. They stared in open-mouthed wonder as Sachin sat down by the microphone. He appeared a bit down and burdened by some deep thoughts. But he greeted the crowd of reporters with a warm smile.

"Good morning and thank you every one for coming. Please be seated and make yourself comfortable," said Sachin.

He turned around to say something to the people sitting on either side of him. They were all pretty serious looking and morose guys in dark suits and ties, probably some very important people. But, for Sam and Fawad, they were as good as non-existent.

"Looks like we have some junior reporters here as well," commented Sachin as he looked back at the crowd. It was then that Sam realized that he was looking at the two of them. So lost were they in the admiration of their idol that they were the only two people still standing.

Sam realized in an instant that this was the opportunity and he came right to the task, "Sir, we are not reporters. We are two cancer patients who have come a long way to see you regarding a very important matter."

Sachin was taken aback by what he was hearing but regained his composure in an instant, "You must be the kids that Murugan told me about, right? Why don't you meet me later, after I am over with this press conference?"

Fawad jumped into the dialogue, "Sir, we would have travelled all this way for nothing if this press meet proceeds the way we fear. We must talk to you now."

Sachin appeared a bit confused as to what the issue was, so were all the reporters gathered there. Finally, after a few minutes, he seemed to have arrived at a decision.

"Fine, let's do it your way; just because I am curious to see where this is going. Why don't you boys come with me? The rest of you, please wait for a few more minutes." Sachin was already up and moving and pointed at Sam and Fawad as he went.

"Yes! We did it," cried the boys in unison as they followed him out of the conference hall. Glancing back, they saw Anu*didi* give them a thumbs-up.

It was up to them now…

****

"Okay, kids. I thought you were after a donation or something like that – Children's Cancer Foundation and all that. What is this really about?" Sachin asked as he hurriedly sat down on the sofa in the sparsely furnished room adjacent to the main conference hall. Sam and Fawad stood in front of him while the rest of the crowd waited outside in the hall.

"Those were all lies we said to meet you. This really is about convincing you to not announce your retirement today," Sam spoke with absolute conviction.

"What! How did you...did Murugan tell you about this?" said Sachin, flabbergasted.

"How can that poor guy know your mind? Unless you discuss your career prospects with your gate keeper," Fawad said. He'd found the question very silly.

"So it means you were planning to retire today, isn't it?" Sam latched on to Sachin's comments and understood their meaning.

"Well, yes, but no, that's not the point. If no one told you, how did you kids know?"

"Sam here has psychic abilities. I myself am a fortune teller," Fawad said, liking the confused expression on Sachin's face and working to compound his misery.

"Shut up, you idiot," Sam said whacking him on the head. "Sorry about Fawad ... he's a lunatic. The truth is we didn't know for sure. But we deduced as much from your general appearance on the TV and your blogs."

"So you boys are telling me that you came here on the hunch that I was going to announce my retirement today?"

"Yes, we saw all those nuts on the TV, the so-called experts, already writing the obituaries for your cricketing career, the newspapers too were lambasting your bad performances in the recent years. We figured they would get to you and make you take a stupid decision. Guess we were right," said Sam resting his case.

"Yes, you were," Sachin sighed as he rested his head in the palms of his hands. All the emotional turmoil of the past few months came rushing in as he sat in silence. This decision had not been an easy one for him. As much as he loved cricket and wanted to keep playing, he could no longer bear to suffer the constant criticism from the media - and this was after he had devoted the better part of his life to his beloved game and his country. But here were two kids now asking him to withdraw from his decision and go back to facing all of that again. He tried to clear his mind by changing the topic.

"Let me clear all this up first. Where are you from?"

"Calicut ... we are patient's at the Palliative Care Centre there," said Sam.

"My goodness! And where are your parents?"

"In Calicut, only," Fawad answered, as though it was quite obvious.

"So how did you reach here? Who are you with?"

"We reached by train. We are with Anudidi, and Munna and Shyam are waiting outside," Fawad.

"Who is Anu didi? Where is she?"

"She is a news reporter. She's out there in the hall."

Sachin was now more confused than ever, "This is getting nowhere. You better tell me everything from the beginning."

Sachin's eyes grew wide in amazement as he listened to the incredible journey these two kids had made overcoming the difficulties of their illness, man-made obstacles and the challenges of this strange and unknown city with their amazing willpower and resourcefulness. And all this just to ensure that *he* could possibly realize his dream of lifting the World Cup.

"What can I say. I am moved," said Sachin as the boys finished their story. Whatever the media might say, there were still countless people like these boys here who wanted him to keep playing. "Breaking out of the hospital was a bad idea though."

"We are sorry for that, but we thought this was the best way to convince you," said Sam.

"Oh, I am convinced alright. You two are very convincing and very special kids."

"See, I told you this would work," said Fawad with glee. "It's not just us though, all the kids in our hospital think the same. Here, we have a letter from them for you." Fawad searched through his bag and finally found what he was looking for – the letter composed by the rest of the kids back home. It was a bit crumpled up from all the manhandling by Fawad but it was readable enough. The contents were a masterpiece in emotional writing, at least that's what Raju had told him when he had handed over the thing.

Sachin took the letter from Fawad and opened it. It was a masterpiece, alright:

From

Raju, Mini, Sam, Fawad, Shreejith, Salim, Anu, Vidya and Faisal (there are others but I can't recollect all of their names)

Different Classes

Calicut

To

The Sachin Tendulkar

Indian Cricket Team

India

***Sub**:- Application for Don't Retiring*

Respected Sir,

We are children from the Hospital in Calicut. We are writing this letter so that you can read this and continue playing cricket. We know that you not scoring many runs now and so people are scolding you. So you become sad and want to retire with cricket.

If you retire now, it will create lots of problems. Fawad will loose his bet and lost five 5-stars. Sam will stop food eating and probably break the TV. This will be very bad as then we cannot be able to watch cartoons. Even Anu and Mini don't want you to retire, even though they don't know anything about cricket.

On the whole, it will be bad for everyone if you retire. Hence, we humbly request you to keep on playing cricket forever, or at least till the World Cup.

Thanking you,

Yours Obediently,

All the above People

P.S: Please come here to meet us if you can. Sam and me are good cricket batsman. We can teach you. Keep drinking Boost; it will give you the energy for playing the WorldCup.

Sachin roared with laughter as he finished reading. Sam and Fawad stood clueless as they were unaware of the contents of the letter but they did know that it was supposed to move him emotionally, not send him into fits of laughter.

When Sachin had recovered sufficiently, he pocketed the letter and got up. "Okay then, you have done your work ... now let me do mine," he said in a serious tone.

"So you won't retire?" Sam asked expectantly.

"No, but let me finish the press meet first."

"But if you are not retiring, what is the need for the press meet?" asked Fawad.

"You will see," said Sachin with a wink.

****

"Sorry for the delay everyone," said Sachin as he took his seat at the dais again. Sam and Fawad too entered the hall and seated themselves next to Anuradha.

"So, how did it go?" she asked

"You will see," Fawad said, repeating Sachin's words. Anuradha wanted to ask more questions but then Sachin had started his speech.

"Over the past few months, there has been increasing speculation in the media that my time is over and that I am retiring. Many of you have probably come here today, expecting me to announce exactly this. All of you must also have already prepared full-length articles and write-ups from famous columnists and sports gurus regarding my career to go along with tomorrow's headlines. The news channels would also have planned for a whole day of interviews and playbacks of my greatest moments."

Sachin took a breather and a sip of water before continuing, "Well, you can dump all those articles, send all those videos back to cold storage and cancel all the interviews, because I am not retiring today or anytime in the near future."

A collective gasp went around the hall, which proved that Sachin was right. It took a few seconds before the commotion died down and Sachin could continue, "God willing, I will be playing with the Indian team in the upcoming World cup and will do everything in my power to win it. That will be all. Thank you and no questions." And with that Sachin got up and left the hall.

A stunned silence followed. Sam and Fawad's face shone with contentment, their mission accomplished. Anuradha was happy for the boys; their journey had been very fruitful. They were the only three happy souls in the hall though; for the rest of them there was lot of work to be done. Headlines had to be changed; new breaking stories had to be generated to make up for the deficit created by Sachin's non-retirement. Some came up and tried to click a few snaps of the two kids who probably had had something to do with Sachin's outburst. But the boys were quickly enveloped by Sachin's personal staff and whisked away, leaving the flustered journos short of another piece of breaking news.

End result: the boys came, saw and conquered without the rest of the world knowing anything about it.

****

Back to Home

"Are you happy, kids?" Sachin asked. They were seated in the same room in which he had met Sam and Fawad earlier. The boys were now seated opposite him along with Anuradha who had been called in at their request.

"Very happy! Now we can return home in peace," said Fawad.

"First things first, we should call your parents and inform them of your whereabouts. They must be worried sick by now," said Sachin.

"Yeah, regarding that – why don't we do it after some time? We are very tired now," Sam said as he looked around. In reality, he wanted to avoid that call. The fact was that they had run away from the hospital and couldn't exactly expect accolades for that. His dad's anger was legendary among his subordinates although he had never been angry with Sam. There's a first time for everything though.

Sachin understood Sam's fears and provided the solution, "Why don't you give me your dad's number and I will call him. He probably won't vent his anger on me."

For Sam and Fawad, nothing could be better. They quickly wrote their mom and dad's phone numbers on a piece of paper and handed it over to Sachin. Sachin dialed a number on his mobile and quietly wandered out of the room as it rang. A few tense minutes later, he came back, handed the phone over to Sam and said, "It's your dad ... talk to him."

Sam took the phone and, with his voice down to almost a whisper, said, "Hello, Dad?" He was expecting a tirade from the other end but was surprised to hear laughter.

"Sam, you silly boy! You actually are with Sachin Tendulkar!" Mr. Martin's voice was a mixture of relief at having found his son and the exhilaration of having talked to Sachin.

With the tension eased, the words flowed from Sam, "Yes, dad. I am sorry we ran away. I also stole your card and took out some money. I think the card is damaged now, it won't work. We are fine and will be back home soon," Sam blabbered as he heard a scuffle at the other end of the line.

"Sam beta, its mom. How are you, son? I have almost died of worry here. Your dad has been blasting away at the hospital staff and anyone who crossed his path. Why am I telling you all that? How are you? Have you had a fever or anything? Did you eat properly?" The questions kept flowing until finally mom started sobbing and stopped.

"I am fine, mom. Don't cry. Just think of it as a school trip – like the one I went to last year for one whole week," Sam said trying to cheer his mom up. But she was proving to be inconsolable.

"Okay, you come back here immediately and then I am not leaving your side ever again," declared his mother. "Sam, is Fawad there? Yes... his Ammi wants to talk to him."

Sam handed the phone over to Fawad and he too faced a crying Ammi who needed much comforting. He also came to know that his dad was already on the way home from Dubai, thanks to his son's exploits.

With that business taken care of, the boys gave Sachin's phone back to him along with another one that Sam produced from his pocket.

"What's this?" asked Sachin.

"It's Murugan uncle's phone. Can you give it back to him?" requested Sam.

"Why? Aren't you coming with me to my house?"

Sam and Fawad looked at each other; it was already past noon and they could not hope to catch the train back to Calicut on the same day. So, they had another day at hand in Mumbai – better to make the most of it.

"We sure would love to..." Fawad began but stopped midway as he thought of something, "We have two friends waiting outside. Can they come too?"

"Sure, let's pick them up on the way then," said Sachin as he started to leave.

"Another thing," Sam interrupted.

"Now what?"Sachin asked with a sigh.

"Can we borrow 500 rupees from you?" asked Sam. He saw Sachin arch his eyebrows in confusion and added, "We promise to return it by money order once we get back to Calicut."

Sachin laughed out loudly; this was the second time today that the boys had managed to do this. Though on both occasions, they themselves had no idea of the reason for the laughter. Sachin was alone though this time; everyone else, including Anu didi had joined in.

"What do you need the money for?" asked Sachin as the laughter died down.

"To buy train tickets," answered Sam.

"I think I can make alternate arrangements for our travel," said Sachin as he ushered them out with a mischievous smile on his face.

Sam and Fawad were left wondering as to the meaning of 'alternate arrangements' and 'our travel'.

****

The journey back home was a breeze compared to their harrowing train experience. For one, it was on a private plane hired by Sachin. And to top it all, the guy himself was coming back with them to Calicut. The meaning of 'alternate arrangements' and 'our travel' had become pretty obvious now.

Fawad had never been on a plane before and was super excited. He couldn't keep still and kept running from one end of the plane to the other. Probably fearing for the safety of the other passengers, the pilots took him into the cockpit where he was more likely to sit still, given the lack of space. In hindsight, this was a big mistake on their part. Fawad harangued them for the remainder of the time it took to reach their destination; he wanted a crash course in piloting.

Sachin was lost in the pages of a magazine at the other end of the plane and so Sam was left alone to dream. He looked back at the events of the day with satisfaction. The best part had been the look on Munna and Shyam's faces when Sachin had asked them to get in his car. They had got in as though in a daze and remained as such till they had reached Sachin's place. Though he had said otherwise, it was written all over his face that Munna was overwhelmed and overjoyed at meeting the man.

"Do you kids want to go to school and live like other kids in a proper home?" Sachin had asked. The question was directed at Munna and Shyam.

The two of them were wary of any change and so were reluctant at first, but a pep talk from Sam and Anu didi did the trick. Plus, you couldn't exactly say no to Sachin. Fawad was averse to the whole idea of schools and hence kept away from all this talk.

Sachin got busy on the phone while the boys roamed around his home; they met up with Murugan who was overjoyed to see them and his phone back. Later, over a hearty lunch, Sachin had informed them of his plans. Sam and Fawad were to leave along with Sachin after lunch while Munna and

Shyam would leave for an NGO centre with which he was affiliated.

As they were parting ways, the iron mask melted away and tears flowed as Munna hugged each of them in turn. "I will never forget you two," he said through the sobs.

"Neither will we," said Sam as he produced a photo from his bag and gave it to Munna, "Here, I want to you to have this."

Munna glanced at the photo and smiled. It showed the two of them chatting away with the Gateway and the Taj in the background. Sam had got this one clicked discreetly from a street photographer.

"Thank you for this and everything else that you have done for us," said Munna.

"No, thank you for helping us out. None of this would have been possible without you," said Sam.

"He's thanking you for something and you are thanking him for something. Why isn't anyone thanking me for anything? I am the hero of this story, after all, isn't it, Anu didi!" Fawad chirped in. He had this gift for resolving awkward emotional situations with his well-thought-out stupid comments. And so everyone said their goodbyes over laughter rather than tears.

An announcement was being made over the plane's speaker system. So lost was he in his thoughts that Sam had lost track of time. He strained his ears to hear Fawad's voice announcing, "Yay, we are in Calicut." As an afterthought he added in a stern voice, "Passengers are advised to put on their seat belts. They are the belt-like things on your seats. I will personally come and throw out anyone who has not put on belt seats, Er… seat belts."

His loose talk aside, Fawad was right about one thing; they were already landing.

They were in Calicut.

Back Home.

****

Friends Forever

Their little escapade had lasted for about four days, but judging from the overwhelming response from their moms, it would seem they had been away for four years. Their parents had been waiting by the runway along with an entourage of cars, probably arranged by Sachin's minions. After having been hugged to death and slobbered with kisses, the boys were now en route to the hospital, with Sachin in the lead. The group had got down, entered the waiting vehicles and left the airport through one of the side routes to avoid possible mass hysteria; it was not every day that Sachin Tendulkar came to Calicut.

"Does doctor uncle know that we are coming?" asked Sam with some trepidation.

"We were in the doctor's office when you first called. So, yes he knows," said his father.

"Is he angry?" This was Fawad.

"Oh no, he is in fact very happy with you two. He was even planning a big reward or something for you," Ammi replied with a grin.

"Really? What is it?" Fawad actually believed his mom.

"Don't know. He said it was a surprise," said Mr. Martin, "But we did see a bag full of needles in his room."

Sam and Fawad looked at each other and gulped. "We are bringing Sachin along with us to his hospital. That should brighten his day," said Sam. He was hoping that doctor uncle would forgive them their mistakes, given this incentive.

The rest of the way back was spent describing the details of their stay in Mumbai and, of course, the meeting with Sachin. The boys also got to know of the happenings back here once it had been discovered that they were missing. A police complaint had been lodged the very next day and they had conducted a detailed but futile interrogation of all the staff in the hospital. One of the kids though had said something about a letter for Sachin and suggested the possibility of Mumbai, but it was dismissed as totally impossible. It seemed that Sam and Fawad had managed to do the impossible.

"We even prepared pamphlets and notices with your pictures on them," said Mr. Martin. "There's a whole bundle of them lying there at the back ... guess we won't be using them anymore."

"Unless you two have something else brewing," said Sam's mom as she looked at the two of them.

"*Aiyobaba,* please don't do anything like this again. I don't think I will be able to handle it," said Ammi as she dramatically folded her hands before the kids.

"Right, so if you have anything similar lined up, please inform me beforehand and I myself will take you there," said Mr. Martin.

"We were actually thinking of the World cup, you know," said Fawad as he flashed Sam with a mischievous smile.

Oh no, thought everyone else in the car.

****

"You seem to be running a slight fever," said Dr. Senthil as he conducted his usual check-up on Fawad. It had been a few months since their Mumbai sojourn and, luckily for them, it had not resulted in any major health issues till now.

"Give him a full CBC and spinal tap along with chest X-rays. Get me the results by the evening," said the doctor, issuing directions for the accompanying nurse before leaving. Sam and Fawad peeped in from the doorway; doctor uncle had gone slightly bonkers ever since the visit from Sachin. Every now and then he could be seen playing imaginary straight drives and square cuts with his stethoscope.

Not just doctor uncle though -Sachin's visit was still fresh in the minds of most people here. He had paid a visit to all the inmates there, greeted everyone with a smile, posed for photos and signed loads of hastily assembled autograph books. The pediatric wing went berserk with joy and laughter when he went there. He chatted away with the kids and gave them loads of goodies that he had brought along. He also gave a special big jar of Boost to Raju, the reason for which was still unclear to Sam and Fawad.

"So boys, can I take a picture of you two before I go?" asked Sachin as he stood in the hospital driveway, waiting for his vehicle to arrive.

"Here, we have one ready," said Fawad as he gave him one of the notices he had picked from the car. It showed the two of them with the words 'Missing' in big bold red letters below.

Sachin smiled as he took the notice, "I will keep this one, but I want another one with all of us together." He came over and stood alongside them and then clicked away with his mobile camera.

"Thank you boys for making me believe in my dream once again," Sachin said as he waved them goodbye.

****

"Boy, the guy seems hell bent on taking his revenge," said Fawad as he lay back on his bed. "They are going to stick me with needles everywhere for whatever he just said now."

"It's for your own good beta," said Ammi as she went to fetch some hot water from the canteen.

"Yes beta, you have to get better before the World cup starts tomorrow," said Sam as soon as Ammi was out of earshot; he was enjoying Fawad's misery.

"Laugh away all you want. I will be having the last laugh though," said Fawad.

"We will see. Hey, do you wanna bet on Sachin scoring his hundredth century during the World cup?"

"I already have that one going with Raju. You can join in if you want. By the way, Sachin called up yesterday to see how we were doing."

"What! Why didn't you call me?" Sam was disappointed at missing Sachin's call.

"Well, you were not here and I was too sick to get out of the bed. Maybe you should move in here with me? There's lots of space around."

"No, thanks. I would rather get needles poked into me all over than have to listen to your chatter all day. What did Sachin say?"

"Nothing much. He's practicing a lot. I gave him a few tips," Fawad said in a self-congratulatory tone.

"Really? That's exactly what he needed. Cricketing tips from the master himself," said Sam sarcastically.

"He also gave me Munna and Shyam's contact number," Fawad added deciding not to take note of Sam's comments.

"Now that's a good thing! Let's call them up now and see how they are doing."

They dialed the number, asked for Munna and Shyam and waited till they heard the familiar gruff voice of Munna at the other end, "Hello, who is this?"

"This is the Police Commissioner ... you are under arrest."

"Mr. Commissioner sir ... you sound very similar to an idiotic boy I met a few months back. Is your name Sam, by any chance?" Munna had instantly recognized Sam's voice.

"Boy, you got me! How are you doing anyway? How's Shyam?"

"Shyam is fine ... he is saying hello to you two. Where's Fawad?"

"He's here and fine for now, but by evening his ass will be full of needle holes. How's the new place?"

"It's fine ... but this school thing is hard. Don't know why people need to study all this *bakwas* anyway!"

"So you can become smart and intelligent like me."

"If I have to study all this then my head at least will start to look like yours – clean as a whistle. Okay, the guy here is signaling that this much chit-chat is enough ... got to get back to class now."

"Okay then. Have fun in school while we enjoy our school-less, dull lives. Give my regards to Shyam. Bye!" Sam hung up.

He had wandered off down the corridor with the phone in his hand. As he came back to into Fawad's room, his heart skipped a beat. Fawad lay with his eyes half-closed as blood dripped down his nose onto his chest. The sheet around him was already stained a crimson color. Sam stood there momentarily paralyzed and then ran down the corridor screaming for the doctor.

****

The World Cup started the next day but Sam had lost all interest. He could hear the roars of joy or the groans of despair whenever he passed by the TV hall but his mind was preoccupied with other things. The other things, of course, meant the condition of Fawad.

Over the course of the next few days, Fawad alternated between recovery and deterioration. He was constantly being wheeled in and out of the ICU, so Sam saw very little of him. Ammi was too busy crying to be of any help. Plus she was now mostly surrounded by a horde of in-laws. Fawad's dad had rushed back from Dubai –a sure sign that something was seriously wrong. This was his second hasty trip in the last few months–the first of course was when the boys went on their little escapade. Sam's questions were mostly never answered properly by the doctors or the nurses. So, he kept himself confined to his room, hoping for the best and fearing the worst.

One day, however, just as Sam was about to retire for his afternoon siesta, Ammi came into the room. Sam's mom asked her to come in but she kept standing by the doorway.

"Sam beta, Fawad is asking for you," she said and broke down in tears. Sam's mom ran over and tried to comfort her but to no avail. Sam jumped out from the bed and ran to Fawad's room with Ammi and his mother following close behind.

His friend was a pale shadow of the lively Fawad Sam was used to. Miscellaneous tubes and IV lines crisscrossed his frail body. But the twinkle in his eyes and the mischievous grin on his face was still there.

"Hey, Sam," he said as Sam came close and held his arms, "Looks like you got your wish ... they have drilled me with needles."

Sam tried to be cheerful for Fawad but could only manage a weak smile back. "It's just that deadly cold again. You will be up and running in no time."

"I think it's slightly more than that this time – multisystem organ failure. Guess I got a fancy sounding disease like yours."

Sam tried to change the topic, "You know, India won today's match and Sachin too scored a lot of runs. We should see the next match together."

"That may prove to be difficult unless you can carry me up to the TV room."

"That's what friends are for," said Sam.

"Sure … friends forever then," said Fawad as he closed his eyes.

The monitor started beeping and a team of doctors and nurses rushed in. They gently pushed Sam out of the way and crowded around Fawad. His family members too moved in and Sam was left with no option but to get out of the room. As he walked back down the empty corridor, he could no longer control his tears.

Yes, Fawad… Friends Forever.

****

A Dream Come True

The D-day had arrived. Excitement intermingled with anticipation pervaded the atmosphere. The very air had a sweet World Cup-ish hint to it. Sam though couldn't feel any of that because he was now breathing through a life-support system. Nothing, not even being hooked to a machine could stop him from watching his team in action. And so a portable TV set was now standing right by his bedside.

His friends and family were gathered around in the room. No one seemed to share his World Cup enthusiasm though. His mother sat in a corner with a morose look on her face and a tired smile on her lips. She was barely managing to hold it together and put up a brave front.

His father was not to be seen in the room. He was, in fact, seated outside it, staring at the ceiling. He couldn't bear to see his little champ like this. His face was a sea of emotions, the likes of which could get him an Oscar, if all this wasn't for real. Anger at the Gods, frustration at his inability to do anything and dejection at the hand fate had dealt him. The fact that India was playing the World cup final was little consolation as far as he was concerned.

Lil' Tony stared at everything around his brother in amazement. This was his first visit to the hospital and, to his tiny eyes Sam was the king of this establishment. There were doctors and nurses darting in from time-to-time, checking on him. An assortment of candies and fruits was laid by his bedside. He even had his own TV, AC and an array of other machines. *Wow, this is the life,* he thought. Sam though didn't seem to be enjoying it much. Probably boredom had crept in. Little did he know what was going on with his brother or what was coming. The meaning of life and the finality of death were beyond his grasp. Good for him. The innocence of childhood and accompanying ignorance is truly bliss.

One person conspicuous by his absence was Fawad. It would have been fun seeing him do his special 'boundary dance'. Yes, he did indeed have a dance for every boundary hit. Though he called it special, the dance mostly involved flailing his arms and legs wildly in the air like a beached whale. Sam wanted to remember Fawad as his happy, cheerful and sometimes idiotic mate. He had insisted on attending Fawad's funeral and was afterwards sorry for it. He definitely didn't want the image of his friend being lowered into a hole in the earth to be his final memory of him. In addition, Sam had got reprimanded by his dad that day. On the way back, he had casually asked his father about what would be done to him when he died. His father had categorically denied discussing his son's funeral plans with him. *Probably better that way,* Sam thought, *it should be a surprise.*

His mind was wandering now. It didn't matter though. The other team was batting. His hero would be in action only later in the evening. He wondered if he could hold on till then. If he died without knowing the end result, he could never be at ease, even in heaven. And Fawad would not stop taunting him for all eternity. Nope, dying was out of question till at least the final ball was bowled. Some form of communication should exist between this world and heaven. He could probably get the result over the Internet there. He hoped Jesus kept himself current with the times.

He had dozed off. By the time he woke up, Sachin had come and gone without any significant contribution. Though team India was slowly but surely closing in on a historic triumph. Breathing was getting a bit difficult. He wanted to hold on though; any moment now, India and Sachin could realize their dream. And so would he.

The moment finally came; India had done it. They were the World champions. The celebrations had begun. The sound of drum beats and fire crackers could be heard outside. Sam felt as though his heart would explode like a fire cracker. The people in the room though were not as overjoyed as him. At least no one was spoiling the occasion by bawling out loud.

He had done it. All the effort that he and Fawad had taken to make sure Sachin played in the World Cup had finally paid off. Sam relived their adventurous journey to meet the very man who was dancing around on TV now like a little boy. Seeing him run around the ground crazy with joy made it all the more worthwhile. Now his team mates were carrying him around on their shoulders. Easy boys, he was already in heaven, no need to actually lift him up to there. The commentators were also babbling on incoherently - probably delirious. *What was that strange noise though?*

A machine near him was beeping loudly. Everyone gathered around his bed. He could make out the faces of his mother and father. Ah, there was Tony. He too looked worried now. However, some idiot was blocking the TV. He tried to ask the guy to move but no sound was coming from his throat.

His mother and father came close, pecked him on the cheek and said their goodbyes. *Hey, I am not dead yet,* thought Sam. The machine was still beeping pretty loudly. What is that strange light though? Someone seemed to be standing at the end of it. Was it Fawad? He couldn't see clearly; it was getting darker by the minute. He wanted someone to make the guy in front of the TV move.

With one mighty effort, Sam opened his eyes one more time. Thankfully, the guy had moved away, so he could see the TV once more. There he was -Sachin - holding onto the World cup trophy. His hero had realized a lifelong ambition and he, Sam, had done his small part in making it come true. The glitter of the World Cup and the gleam in Sachin's eyes was the last thing that Sam's eyes took in before they shut forever.

Both Sachin and Sam were now at peace…

****

Epilogue

"In hindsight, that is the story of how three cancer patients helped Sachin Tendulkar realize his destiny," Mr. Martin said, winding up his story. "The world, of course, knows about only one of them and thankfully he is alive."

"The world will soon know about the other two ... this I promise you," said Anuradha as she wrapped up her stuff. She offered her condolences to Sam's mom, took a final look at his pictures adorning one wall of the house and left.

Mr. Martin too looked up at the photos, specifically the one that showed Sam and Fawad standing together, hand in hand. Theirs was a friendship that had been pure and unadulterated by any feelings of personal gain. It had helped them overcome the limitations imposed by their disease and influenced so many lives during their brief but momentous journey.

They had helped Sachin, of course. Sachin, in turn, had taken over the responsibility for Munna and Shyam. He got them off the streets and into a proper school. The Palliative Centre had benefitted tremendously from Sachin's benevolence; Dr. Senthil was a happy man. They had brought joy to the otherwise dreary and painful lives of the countless patients in that hospital.

All in all, a life well lived. Well done, my boys. I am really proud of you, thought Mr. Martin.

****